THE GOLDEN PECKER

PENELOPE BLOOM

1

ANDI

Well, that sucked.

I thought about going back to the hotel lobby where my sisters were grieving but decided against it. We had all spent the past few days moping, and the only way I'd start piecing my life back together was to do normal things. Like eating too much candy and reading books. Alone, preferably.

I shuffled down the checkered carpet hallway in my fluffy socks, not paying particular attention to where I was going. After all, my sisters and I had grown up in this hotel. I probably could've made the trip to the vending machine blindfolded.

I passed a row of frost-covered windows that gave me a glimpse of yet another snowy New York City night. Thankfully, the heat in the hotel was cranked up so I was plenty comfortable in my thin sweater and socks. Of course, I also stood out like a sore thumb. The Wainwright hotel was a five-star establishment where most of the women I passed were decked out in designer outfits and the men wore tailored, thousand-dollar suits.

Good for them. All I cared about was getting a bag of Skittles and diving into a book to distract myself.

I left the window and went into the small room where the

vending machines were. I rarely saw any of the rich guests lowering themselves to using the machines, but tonight, there was a man inside the small room.

He had short, messy hair and a face that belonged on some long-dead dark prince. It was all graceful lines and sharp edges, with strong eyebrows over a pair of equally dark, piercing eyes. I guessed he might be in his early thirties but couldn't be sure.

I hadn't been self-conscious about my casual clothes until I saw him looking me up and down.

"Nice socks," he said.

I was a little startled that he was speaking to me. I'd never had much luck with men, and I'd never even spoken to a guy on this man's level. "Wasn't planning on going out, so..." I said, trailing off.

He noticed the Kindle tucked under my arm. "Long night of reading?"

"Something like that."

"What are you reading?"

"Uh," I said, face turning a bright red. *Just make something up. Think of anything. Any normal book that won't embarrass you.* "Uh..."

A slow smile spread across his lips. *They were nice lips, too.* "Here," he said, reaching to take it from under my arm.

All sorts of internal alarms went off. *Danger. Bad. Very bad.* All I could do was stand there in stupid shock, watching as he tapped the screen and woke up my Kindle—the one I'd never bothered to password protect.

The man's eyebrows shot up. "Wow. This is quite the library." His face scrunched up when he noticed something, then he burst out with a deep chuckle. "*The Cocktopus?* Any chance you can give me a plot summary on that one?"

A sound somewhere between "dying cat" and "old, rusty door" escaped from my lips. "I can explain that."

He made a carefree gesture, handing the Kindle back to me.

"You look embarrassed," he said seriously. "Don't be. Too many people are ashamed of what they desire. I've never believed in hiding from what we want."

Now it was my turn to raise my eyebrows. Was he making a pass at me?

"See," I said, talking more to fill the silence than for any other reason. "I don't always read the title of books. I got started on that one, and then the hero got some irradiated goo on his... *Yeah.* And before I knew it, I was reading a story about the dreaded octocock and his sexual exploits."

"You like reading on those things more than paperbacks?" He asked, gesturing to the Kindle.

"I've kind of always hoped I'd become a writer some day, so I read a lot. And my Grandpa thought this would be easier than always having to walk to the store. Actually though, walking to the store and smelling the books and just... being around all of that. It's part of the magic for me. So, no," I said, turning over the Kindle and looking at it. "But he gave it to me, and it feels like that's more important right now, I guess?"

The man listened to me go about ten miles deep into the T.M.I with a stranger zone like I was the most interesting person he'd ever met. His eyes hardly moved from mine, and the way he seemed so fascinated was an odd combination of flattering and unnerving. "So you want to write?" he asked. The shadow of a smile crossed his mouth. "I wonder if the stories in your head are as dirty as the ones on that thing?"

I clamped my mouth shut tightly. Some girls blushed when they got embarrassed. Others shut down and got quiet. But me? I felt an almost compulsive need to say something sarcastic or funny to diffuse the moment. It was far from my most charming quality, and I'd already decided I wasn't going to make a bad impression on this guy. With an effort, I forced myself to say something normal, even if it was a few beats too slow to sound natural. "I just like writing. It doesn't even have to be a story, so..."

"Well," he said. "I won't know to keep an eye on the shelves for you unless I know your name. I'm Landon, by the way. Landon Collins."

"Andi Wainwright," I said, reaching to shake his hand.

The warm look on his face abruptly changed and he paused before taking my hand in his. "Wainright," he said slowly. "As in the granddaughter of the man who owned this hotel?"

Owned. Past tense. As in, Grandpa Willy is dead, remember? But hey, I was an old pro when it came to the death of loved ones. At least I didn't need to delude myself into thinking it would get better with time. No I'd learned that time just helps you find ways to avoid thinking about it for long enough periods of time to function.

"Uh," I said, stammering a little when I realized I'd just been staring back at him like an idiot. "Yes. That's me."

Landon's nostrils flared.

It was like a switch had flipped. Even though I couldn't put my finger on what it was, something in his expression had hardened, wiping away all the approachability and kindness I'd seen just a few moments ago. It was almost like learning I was Grandpa Willy's granddaughter was some sort of problem in his mind. I couldn't imagine why. Before he died, my grandpa had gotten along with everyone I ever saw.

He turned back to the machine and tapped the same button a few times, then grunted with irritation.

"Here," I said, stepping forward. I kicked the leg at the front of the machine and pulled my foot back quickly. The leg slid backwards, making the machine fall slightly and jostle his candy free.

Landon gave me an unreadable look, then dug out the bag. He held it up to me and gave a little shrug. "My dad always loved the things," he said.

"My grandpa did, too," I said. I stuck my coins in the machine and tapped the number to get a bag for myself. "He always had them around. Practically grew up on the-" when I turned, Landon was gone, and I was talking to myself.

Instead of reading alone, I met my sisters in the lobby. Bree was working on college applications and Audria was scribbling notes by hand for her dissertation.

Bree noticed me first. She had dirty blonde hair, light brown eyes, and was pretty in a painfully sweet kind of way. She looked up, smiling but clearly scanning me for any signs of distress. Even though she was the youngest of us at eighteen, she had a habit of trying to mother us.

I smiled back, doing my best not to let any of my feelings show so she'd leave it alone. I plopped into an armchair next to Audria, who was sitting cross-legged on the carpet.

If Audria knew how to wipe the scowl from her face, she would've had the same kind of sweet prettiness Bree had. Instead, she wore her black hair in a tight ponytail and always seemed to be thinking about something deep and concerning.

For a few minutes, all I did was sit in the chair and stare at my Kindle. I didn't even turn it on. I just looked down at the black screen like if I stared hard enough, I could feel Grandpa Willy in there. I let out a sigh and hugged the Kindle to my chest, closing my eyes. When my mom and dad died, I lived in the pain until it felt like I didn't even know what was going on around me anymore.

This time, I was trying so damn hard to just keep looking forward. I still hated how I'd done exactly what my mom and dad wouldn't have wanted. I'd let their death paralyze me and wasted years of my life feeling sorry for myself. Of course, Grandpa Willy had been the biggest part of me climbing out of that hole. He adopted us, became like family, and let us know someone still cared.

Except now he was gone, too. There wasn't anyone left to save me, so I needed to do better this time. To *be* better. Even if it was going to hurt, I was going to keep pressing forward and I wasn't going to let his death define me. I also made a silent promise to myself to really give the writing thing a shot, even if I had no idea where to start with that.

"So," Audria said, not looking up from her notes. "I talked to Grandpa's lawyers this morning. There's some sort of weird stipulation in his will, and we have to have it explained to us by a third party."

"Wait," I said. "That doesn't make sense."

Audria shrugged. "Did anything Grandpa Willy did ever really make sense?"

She had a point. "When are we supposed to meet this guy?"

"Any minute," Audria said. "His name is Landon Collins, apparently."

"Uhh," Bree said. "Is she okay?"

Both my sisters were studying me.

"You look kind of... *not okay*," Audria said. "Constipation again? I've told you a million times you need to keep up with the fiber. It's not just something you do when you feel like it, it's-"

"No," I said. I shook my head. "It's just that I already met him. At the vending machine."

Bree squinted. "You guys exchanged names?"

"Yeah, and he looked like he wanted to murder me with an axe when he heard mine. For some reason, I don't think we're going to like whatever he has to tell us."

2

LANDON

I tossed the bag of Skittles in the trash. My father's death had me feeling stupidly sentimental, I guess. I hadn't eaten the things in years.

I was waiting just outside the lobby where I was supposed to meet the Wainwright sisters—Andi, in particular. But I'd accidentally gotten a jump on that directive, hadn't I?

Even though I wasn't sure I'd ever come face to face with the Wainwright sisters, I'd always known how the encounter would go. I'd hate them. It wouldn't matter if they were Kindergarten teachers, charity workers, or the hottest damn women on the planet. I'd hate them purely out of principal, just like I had from afar for most of my life.

Meeting Andi unexpectedly hadn't been part of the plan. But it was just a quick conversation. Sure, I hadn't hated her. I'd even enjoyed the little exchange, but I was certain I could put it all behind me once I'd had a little more time. After all, hating people was much easier than the alternative, and God knew I had plenty of practice.

I raked a hand through my hair and tried to refocus. The

Wainwright sisters were the enemy, I reminded myself. Even Andi. *Especially Andi.*

Fuck it.

I walked into the lobby, spotted them all gathered around a pair of armchairs in the corner, and headed toward them.

Andi was facing me with her head down as she read something on her Kindle—probably one of the many trashy novels I'd seen in her library. She had a simple look about her—with brown hair, brown eyes, an upturned nose, and a slightly too-wide smile. And yet I'd found it hard to look away from her. Maybe it was just the effortlessness about her. She'd been wearing an "I don't give a shit" outfit, didn't appear to be doused in makeup, and probably hadn't spent more than a few seconds on her hair. She'd felt real. Far more real than the women in my life.

Her youngest sister was in the chair across from her. She had the pretty, innocent teacher's pet kind of look about her. A black-haired Wainwright sister sat on the floor cross legged. She was glaring at something in her lap.

Andi looked up when I stopped in front of them. It looked like she wanted to say something but couldn't quite figure out how to word it. Instead of giving her the chance, I started talking.

"Your grandfather asked me to come," I said. "I'm Landon Collins. I just need Andi to come with me."

"What?" asked the black-haired one. I'd never let myself look up pictures of the girls, but I knew Audria was the oldest, and undoubtedly the one sitting on the ground. "Why just her?"

"My job isn't to answer all your questions. Andi can come with me and find out what she needs to do to get her share of the hotel, or she can stay here and get nothing. Simple as that."

All three of them were glaring at me now. *Good.* This was more like the way I'd imagined meeting them would go. Hostility. Anger. The way it should be.

"How do I know you're not a serial killer?" Andi asked.

"I had you alone just a few minutes ago. I could've done whatever I wanted with you." I inwardly cringed at the way the words sounded once they left my lips. I *had* imagined what it would be like to do a few things to her before I'd heard her name. Pinning her against the wall and tasting her with a kiss, for starters. Tying her wrists together with those fluffy pink socks...

"Where am I supposed to go?" Andi asked.

"Downstairs, to The Golden Pecker."

The girls exchanged a look, then burst out laughing.

"What?" Andi asked. "If that's a joke, I don't get it."

I stared. "He never told you about it?" I shook my head. "Never mind. It doesn't matter. You can come with me now, or not. Your choice."

"You're sure the lawyers said his name was Landon?" Andi asked Audria.

Audria nodded.

Andi looked back up at me. "I'm going to assume my Grandpa wouldn't have asked someone to take me to the basement if he thought there was a chance it'd lead to my murder. So, I'm trusting him, not you."

"Great. As long as we can get moving," I said, gesturing for her to follow me.

"You sure this is a good idea?" the youngest sister—Bree, I was fairly sure—asked.

"No," Andi said.

"Here." Audria dug in her bag. She pulled out a small, black object and squeezed the side of it. We all jumped a little when electricity crackled and flickered between the two metal tips on top of it. "It's my taser. Just in case."

3

ANDI

I followed Landon down to the basement of the hotel. I probably should've been more worried for my safety, but I did have the taser Audria had given me. I also believed what I'd said: Grandpa apparently asked this guy to take me somewhere, and I knew he wouldn't have ever put me in danger. I also thought that curling into the fetal position in my room didn't line up with my plan to keep living my life. A little risk and adventure would be good for me.

My plan was to keep my mouth shut. Mostly, I didn't want to give Landon the satisfaction of thinking I was curious or that his rudeness had gotten to me. Whatever his reasons were for flipping a switch and deciding to turn cold, I wasn't going to worry about it.

Except it wasn't that easy. I lasted about two minutes before I finally spoke up in the stairwell.

"What is the story with you and my grandpa?" I asked. "That has to be it, right? You got all pissy toward me when you heard my last name because you knew Grandpa Willy."

He shot me a glare over his shoulder but kept walking.

"Or maybe you stayed at the hotel one night and got a dirty room?" I suggested.

Landon stopped at the door leading to the basement and turned to face me. "Do you always ask so many questions?"

It was so bizarre. Before we exchanged names, he was so easy to talk to. I couldn't have even imagined him having a temper. Now he was acting like a totally different person.

"When strange men make me follow them to the basement, I've been known to get inquisitive."

"Your grandfather and I were business partners." Landon made no attempt to mask the irritation in his voice.

I narrowed my eyes. "That doesn't make sense. I'd have known you if you worked with him. He always introduced me to his friends."

"Clearly not. He never even told you about The Golden Pecker. Besides, we weren't friends. Not even close."

I mulled over the new information while we made our way through the basement and toward the wine cellar. "And what kind of business is The Golden Pecker, exactly?"

"I imagine you'll find out soon enough."

I silently mocked his words to his back while we walked. *Bastard.* I bet he thought he sounded so cool and mysterious. All I knew was that my initial impression of him had been dead wrong. He wasn't a good guy. He was an asshole who was willing to let his grudge with my grandpa trickle down to me.

We reached the far wall of the basement, which was lined from floor to ceiling with wine racks. Most of them were full of bottles, but Landon was eyeing an empty space as he fished for something in his pocket. He pulled out a keychain with a sculpted gold penis and balls about the size of his hand dangling from the end of it.

"Uh," I said slowly.

He held up the key, then looked at it like he hadn't properly noticed it in a while. "Your grandfather was always very mature," he said. He'd looked amused for a moment, then seemed to forget he was supposed to be angry. Landon turned his back to me, stuck the penis in an empty slot on the rack, and twisted it.

There was a metallic click. He pulled on the wine rack and the entire thing slid open, revealing that it was a false wall.

I stared in disbelief. The opening led to a narrow hallway painted black and lined with candles. It looked like the kind of place Vlad the Impaler would've considered a totally sweet entrance to his bachelor pad.

"Have you guys heard of electricity?" I asked. "I hear it's a lot easier than keeping a few dozen candles lit in some obscure underground hallway."

"It's something I might have mentioned to your grandfather a time or two."

I smiled to myself. He wasn't very good being angry, I decided. I could tell that's exactly what he was trying to do. Maybe that should've made me irritated with him, but it only made me curious.

"In here," he said, gesturing me through a doorway.

I had to squeeze past him to get into the room. In an effort to make it less awkward, I turned my back to him, which only made things worse. My ass brushed right across his crotch. I stared wide-eyed at the wall, and then did my best to pretend nothing had happened.

The room was set up like a private theater with about twenty plush leather chairs all arranged in a semi-circle around a huge projector screen. I twirled slowly, taking the place in. "So, The Golden Pecker is what, like a movie theater? Is this one of those porn theaters like in old movies?" I took a step back from the seats when I thought of desperate, grunting old men pleasing themselves while watching erotic films on the screen.

"No," Landon said. "This is just one room. The club is..." He stopped talking and cleared his throat. "Grab a seat and I'll start the video."

I looked at the seats and shook my head. "I think I'll stand."

"Suit yourself," Landon said. He moved behind a console with what I assumed were controls for the projector. He pressed a few buttons, and then the machine whirred into action.

A huge image of my Grandpa Willy filled the screen. It had only been four days since he died but seeing him again felt surprisingly strange. He was smiling, and the bandage on his forehead told me this video hadn't been filmed long before his death.

My heart wrenched at the sight of him. I couldn't help thinking about how strange death was—that one moment, someone could be alive and well with all the invisible little threads that connected them to the world. I liked to think the thread between Grandpa Willy and I had been one of the thickest. But then the fire could just go out inside someone. One moment, they were in there, alive and well. The next, it was just a body.

Maybe that should have made me feel depressed. Instead, all I felt was my own fire burning brighter. Like all the death I'd seen so close just made me realize how important it was to do something with my life while I had it. It might even be part of what always fascinated me about writing. As long as my writing was still being read, I wouldn't ever really be gone.

"This video is for Andi," he said, looking off to the side more like he was making a note for himself than for me. He fixed his eyes on the camera and his expression changed—blossoming into a happy smile. "Welcome to The Golden Pecker! You're probably wondering what the hell this place is. Oh, and if you're sitting in one of those chairs, I'd make sure Landon properly cleaned them first." He laughed. "It's strange, knowing he's there with you. Well, I guess it's also possible that you refused to listen to him, and nobody will ever see this video, but I'll assume that's not the case."

"Anyway," Grandpa continued. "I'm rambling. One of the dangers of getting old, I'm afraid. Welcome to my secret BDSM club." He paused, lips curling at the corners in amusement. Then he waggled his eyebrows up and down a few times. "*Surprise!*"

I turned to look at Landon for confirmation. He spread his hands and gave a little shrug.

"The reason I asked you to come down here is simple and complicated," Grandpa said. "But I'm just going to make this as simple as I can. I want to leave a third of my hotel to you. I also want to leave The Golden Pecker to you. But there's a catch."

I turned again, and the look on Landon's face told me he was hearing all this for the first time, too.

"Now," Grandpa said. "I could explain exactly what my plan is. I could go into all sorts of details and unravel the maniacal genius of this little arrangement and what I hope it'll accomplish, but... *But* I'm afraid the only way this will work is if I keep you two in the dark. Just understand this: Yes, what I'm about to ask you is incredibly strange and probably highly inappropriate, considering I've been like a grandfather to you for so many years."

I waited for him to say more. *But it's not what it sounds like*, or *but I can explain*. Instead, he just smiled and shrugged, continuing.

"You will get a third of my hotel and the club if you complete a little to-do list I'm about to read. If you don't, it all goes to Landon Collins."

I felt lightheaded. When I looked at Landon, he was scowling at the screen in utter confusion. I turned back, letting out a few ragged breaths. *To Landon?* I felt like I'd just watched a cute little old lady on her way out of church drop a few F-bombs. The only thing stopping me from storming out of the room was that I hadn't even heard the to-do list yet. I took a few steadying breaths, trying to force a calm I didn't feel.

I didn't even care about the inheritance. I cared about the fact that my Grandpa was making me feel more and more like I didn't even know him. First, some mysterious grudge with a gorgeous man I've never met? Then a secret BDSM club, and now he was dangling my inheritance in front of me and threatening to snatch it away.

He pressed his lips together in an apologetic smile. "I can practically see the face you're making right now, Andi. Believe me, I wish I could just lay it all out for you and explain this plain as day. Except I can't. It's like I said, the only way this works is if you two are confused as hell. So I'm going to just get to the list. Number one, watch a show in The Red Room. Two, experience bondage. Three, spend an hour in the sensory deprivation chamber. And four—this is the fun one—I want you to spend an entire night as Landon's submissive. The real deal, too. All the bells and whistles." He smiled, almost like he could see the disbelief and disgust on my face. "I know, super creepy. But hey, I've spent a large part of my life building three of the city's most successful BDSM sex clubs. On the spectrum of perverted things I've done, this barely registers. And if you completely hate me right now, I think I'll live. *Oh wait.* No, apparently I didn't!" Grandpa laughed at his own joke.

"Is he serious?" I asked Landon.

Landon shook his head. He didn't look even slightly amused. His eyes were practically burning holes in the screen.

"So," Grandpa said. "I think that wraps it up. Oh. Last thing. Having a team of lawyers tag along to confirm that you complete the list would kind of make it awkward. So I'm putting my complete trust in you, Landon. You're the only one with the authority to say whether Andi completed the list or not."

Grandpa tapped his chin thoughtfully, then held up his finger. "Almost forgot! Landon, you're most likely planning to do

whatever you think would've pissed me off the most. But I did
want to leave you with one mysterious nugget of information.
Finish my list, and you'll get a reward far greater than the club or
money. Ignore the list, and you'll always have to wonder what the
surprise might have been. *Hmm, very mysterious.* Anyway, I'd
better get back to being dead."

The video abruptly cut off. Anger and outrage still churned
inside me. My brain was still playing catchup—trying to confirm
that I'd really heard everything I just thought I did.

I had to do all of those things or my entire inheritance went to
a man I'd just met. There was no way that could be right.
Could it?

"I didn't even understand half of what was on that list," I said
quietly.

Landon gave no sign that he'd heard me.

"And he expects me to do all this weird, perverted stuff with
you? What are you, his henchman?" My voice was getting louder
as I spoke until I was almost yelling.

"I'm not a henchman," Landon said. "I have two degrees from
Yale in business and marketing."

"Okay. He expects me to do all this weird, perverted stuff with
his highly educated henchman?"

Landon ran his thumb across his stubble, then our eyes met.
"I need to think about this."

"What do you mean?" I asked.

"I mean your grandfather just told me the only thing I need to
do to claim my share of a multi-million-dollar hotel and the club
I spent most of my life building is lie to the lawyers. If I say you
refused to attempt the list, it's all mine, right?"

I could only stare. That was how grandpa had made it sound.
"And that's what you're going to do?" I asked quietly. "Ignore what
he wanted and lie to the lawyers?"

He walked toward the doorway and stopped without turning.

"I haven't decided. But if this is the last time I see you, have a nice life, Andi Wainwright."

"No wonder he hated you," I yelled after him. It was a blind guess, but I was grasping at anything I could to sting Landon back, even if it was just slightly.

He paused, head down. I thought he was going to say something, but after a few heartbeats, he stepped out into the hallway and left.

BREE AND AUDRIA WERE WAITING UP FOR ME IN THE LOBBY WHEN I returned. All told, I'd only been gone about half an hour, which seemed hard to believe. It felt like my understanding of the world had been turned on its head, and an hour hadn't even passed.

"That look on her face isn't a good sign," Bree said. She stood from the armchair she'd been sitting in.

Audria was still cross legged on the ground. She looked up from her notepad with a hint of interest. "What happened?"

I explained the entire encounter to them, leaving out the parts where I was embarrassingly attracted to the guy who clearly didn't mind screwing me out of my inheritance. I may have also embellished a few moments here and there, just to make him sound worse.

"That doesn't make sense," Bree said.

"Yeah. That's what I said," I groaned. Little by little, my anger and outrage were cooling. I didn't *want* to be mad at grandpa. His death was still so fresh in my mind that it felt wrong. "But he must have some kind of plan. I mean, he said as much. Maybe I'll understand if I actually go through with the list?"

"You're considering it?" Audria asked. She was looking at me like I was insane.

"Yes," I said. "It was his dying wish."

"That's a little dramatic," Audria said.

"How? He literally wished it right before he died. *Dying wish.* Textbook example."

Bree nodded slowly. "She does have a point. That sounds a lot like a dying wish to me, Audria."

"It doesn't sound like it'll matter if you choose to do the list or not," Audria said. "This Landon guy is just going to go to the lawyers and cut you out of the equation."

"Not if I woo him." I frowned at my own suggestion. "Okay, scratch that. I'm not going to try to woo the guy, but I can at least go find him and try to talk some sense into him."

"I wonder if there are going to be videos for us, too," Bree said.

"Probably. And I have no idea why it's starting with me. I mean, other than the obvious fact that I was Grandpa's favorite."

"Yeah," Audria said. "He liked you so much that he pretty much told a supervillain to take your inheritance unless you go on a sexual scavenger hunt with him."

"What about the thing you said," Bree asked. "Didn't he promise Landon some kind of greater reward if he got you through the list?"

"Yeah," I said. "But what would you choose? A sure thing, or some vague promise from a man you apparently hated more than Paula Deen hates the idea of cooking without butter?"

"I don't know," Bree said. "But the mystery would drive me crazy."

"I think he'll manage," Audria said. "So, are you really going to go try to talk to him?"

"I don't know what else to do," I said.

"Wouldn't you need to know where he is to convince him?" Audria asked.

"Kind of," I admitted. "But I know where the club is. He said he had been helping Grandpa Willy run it. Wouldn't it make sense for him to go back there at some point tonight?"

"You said he had some kind of cock key. Could you even get in without it?"

"That can't be the only way in," I said. "If it's a real club with lots of people, then there's a front entrance. Otherwise, we'd have known about it a long time ago when a constant stream of leather-clad BDSM enthusiasts were parading down to the basement every day."

"Good point," Audria said.

I pulled my hair back into a ponytail and put on my game face. "It's time for me to do some detective work. Also, it's time for me to raid my closet for a convincing outfit to get into a sex club."

"Or," Audria said. "You could just let me pick the lock. If a giant cock was the key, then it's not a normal lock. I bet you could stick almost anything in there and get it to open."

"I'm open to suggestions," I said.

Audria unzipped her bag and fished around for a few seconds. She pulled out a floppy, purple dildo with a suction cup on one end.

Bree and I both clapped our hands over our eyes and groaned.

"Jesus," I said. "Would you stop waving that thing around? And why is it in your school bag? What does—just—"

"Don't worry. I keep it washed and sanitized. It's perfectly sterile," Audria said, as if *that* was our primary concern.

"It's more about the mental image," I said. "And you probably fantasize about cell samples or beakers and Bunsen burners. *Oh,*" I mimicked. "Results would indicate this method of insertion is highly desirable. *Oh!*" I groaned again.

Audria shoved it back in her bag and stood. "Are you going to take me down there and show me the hole, or not?"

"Yes," I said. "But I need to go to my room and change first.

I walked into the club wearing the most aggressively conservative outfit I could find. Black turtleneck, thick, baggy black jeans, and even my most padded, ill-fitting bra. The strategy was simple: be invisible.

All I wanted to do was bust in the place, talk some sense into Landon, and get out.

Audria's dildo had worked in the keyhole, but my sisters decided to hang back and let me do this alone.

I was in the hallway lit by candles again. There was an ominous, lacquered black door at the other end. To my left, the theater room where I'd watched grandpa's video was empty, but the lights were still on and the projector hummed quietly.

I took a steadying breath and moved to the black door, pulling it open.

Quiet, sensual music washed over me.

I was looking at a large, circular room. Everything I could see was dark paneled wood, leather, or satin. It felt like a porn set for vampires.

The space was choked with people. The dress code took about a millisecond to figure out. The women wore as little as they could—from strategically placed dental floss to nearly transparent dresses sans underwear. The men wore suits—thank God.

I spotted Landon sitting at the bar. Behind him, hundreds of bottles of liquor were lit with scarlet light. It had the effect of outlining his broad shoulders in a kind of red glow that I found quite appropriate—considering he was literally the devil.

I walked right up to him and tapped his shoulder. He only showed me how shocked he was to see me for a split second before smoothing his features.

"Wow," he said. He was sitting casually in a bar stool beside a glass of ice water.

What kind of guy sits at the bar and drinks water?

I did a little shrug. "I know. I look fantastic."

"No. I was going to say, if this is your idea of dressing to fit in..."

I resisted the urge to tug at my collar, which felt like it was trying to choke the life out of me. "This is my idea of making sure nobody mistakes me as part of *this*," I said, gesturing to my left and nearly judo chopping a bare boob. I quickly locked my gaze on Landon's so I didn't have to make eye contact with the practically nude woman to my side.

"It's a breast," he said calmly. "I can ask her to let you take a closer look, if you're curious."

"The only thing I'm curious about is what the hell this is doing beneath my Grandpa Willy's hotel. And how it could be here for my whole life and nobody ever told me. And why—"

"The breast, or the club?" he asked.

"The club, smartass."

"Maybe your grandfather wasn't as honest and open as you thought. *Maybe* there were a few skeletons in his closet." Landon looked up with a surprising amount of fire in his eyes. "I wonder if you're the kind of person who would rather dig them up or bury them to preserve his precious memory?"

I wasn't sure why, but I sensed that the question wasn't just a casual one—as if Landon was going to make some sort of decision based on how I responded. "I'm the type of person who is interested in the truth, no matter how much it stings."

"I wonder if you mean that," Landon said.

"What about you?" I asked. "If my grandfather is going to give my inheritance to a man I know nothing about, I'd at least like to know why. Why you? Who were you to him?"

Landon looked at his glass of water and drew his eyebrows together. "That would be the inconvenient truth—the one I'm not sure you're ready for. I'll just say this—the club should've been left to me. I'm the one who worked my ass off to make it what it is. The hotel? Fine. If he wanted to give it to you and your sisters, I wouldn't have cared."

"What are you saying?"

"Complete his list, and you can have your share of the hotel. But the club is mine."

I considered what he'd said, licking my lips. "And if I don't complete the list?"

"Then I keep it all."

I clenched my teeth. The red light from the bar washed his face, making him seem even more sinister. He could've been talking about keeping a quarter he found on the road for all he seemed to care.

"Why?" I asked. "You said it yourself. All you'd need to do is spin a story for the lawyers. So the list is completely irrelevant. My grandfather went to the trouble of making that video, creating all these crazy stipulations, but in the end, all you have to do is lie."

"Maybe. But let me ask you this. What would happen if I gave you your share of the hotel, no questions asked?"

"We could both get out of each other's lives as fast as possible."

Landon leaned in. "And what if that's not what I want?"

My breath caught. Part of me was flattered that he wasn't ready to see me walk away. The other part of me was pissed off.

Then again, I wasn't going to lie. I was so curious it hurt. The writer in me was drawn to mysteries, and Landon was a big, sexy mystery of the highest order. It was the kind of brain food writers dreamed about. Worse, even if I hadn't begun to understand *why*, this was something Grandpa Willy had asked me to do. It was the last thing he'd asked me to do, and the only way I'd ever figure out why was if I faced it.

"Let's say I'm considering this," I said. "What stops you from lying even if I do complete the list? How do I know you'll still give me my share of the hotel?"

"I don't need it, for starters. The club is basically a money printing machine. If that's not enough, well, tough luck, I guess. Either you play along and accept the risks, or you don't play at all. Only one option ends with the possibility that you get what you want."

I glared.

This was it. Option one was walking away and never looking back. Option one also involved the high likelihood that I'd always feel like I let grandpa down somehow. Also wondering if I would've ever found a way to break through the disguise Landon had started wearing when he found out who I was—to find my way back to the guy I'd caught a tantalizing glimpse of by the vending machines.

Option two, on the other hand...

"Show me The Red Room."

Landon laughed, then looked back at his water and shook his head. "Funny."

"I'm serious. Take me there."

He cocked an eyebrow and considered me. "You really want to do this?"

"Take me there," I said, trying to sound more confident than I felt.

Landon turned and nudged a man who was sitting beside him—a man I hadn't noticed until now because he moved about as much as a statue. The man was *big,* even compared to Landon, who was already taller than average. He had a proud nose that gave him a vaguely hawk-like appearance. His hair was black, and his skin was somewhat pale. I thought he had the look of a tortured artist type on steroids—like a young Leonardo DiCaprio mixed with Adam Driver.

"What?" asked the man in a frighteningly deep voice.

"I'm taking this one to The Red Room. Keep an eye on things for me, will you?"

The man looked around, as if asking what Landon expected him to need to monitor.

"Just do it, James," Landon said. "Andi," he gestured to me, standing. "Let's go."

"Wainwright?" James' face was expressionless, but something in his cold eyes seemed to twinkle.

"I don't want to hear it," Landon barked.

He focused his attention on me again and stuck his arm out like he wanted me to play princess and let him escort me.

"No, thanks," I said.

Landon kept his arm out. "Either you let people think you're mine for now, or someone will try to take you for themselves. It's your choice."

I almost cracked a joke, but the look on his face told me he wasn't kidding. Grudgingly, I hooked my arm around his and let him lead me deeper into the club. I could sass him all I wanted, but the truth was I didn't want to wind up as Captain Leather-beard's booty for the night. Not that following Grandpa Willy's list with Landon, AKA Captain Stick Up His Ass, was going to be much better.

Once we left the bar area, the club turned into a labyrinth of tight hallways, dark silk-covered doorways, and confusing turns. It was only twenty seconds before I'd lost my way. I was also finding it hard to focus with the way everybody was looking at us.

At first, I thought it must've been my head-to-toe black clothing and lack of nipple pride. But I quickly realized it seemed like my arm around Landon's was drawing the murmurs and stares.

"Am I missing something?" I asked.

"A lot of things. Tact, for starters. Obedience. A general sense of restraint... I could go on, if you like."

I shot him a dry look. "I mean about why everybody is whispering when they see us."

"You're welcome to worry about whatever you please. It doesn't make a difference to me."

I distantly wondered how cocky he'd sound if I headbutted him in the balls. Then again, I guessed putting my face between his legs in any capacity should probably stay out of my plans. There was a confusing sort of energy with Landon. Sure, I found him to be very punchable. But at the same time... There was this annoying, *very, very* faint intrigue about him. I had questions, and I hated how badly I wanted answers to them. Why was James about as friendly as Darth Vader? Why did Grandpa Willy never tell me about Landon? Why was there a goddamn BDSM club underneath my grandpa's hotel? And, most presently, why was everybody staring like me being on his arm was the scandal of the century?

I can worry about whatever I please, I thought, fuming. Maybe he was the one who should worry that all my violent fantasies would eventually come to life.

"Here we are," he said, pulling back a red curtain that led to a darkened room lined with leather couches, chairs, and even tables set with plates and glasses.

"Very sexy vibe in here," I said. "At least, if you find things like depressing, leather-clad caves sexy."

"Do you always do that?" he asked.

"What?"

"Make jokes when you're nervous?"

"Uh, actually, I get a sick stomach when I'm nervous. So, *no.* Nice try, though." As if my stomach was playing for the wrong team, it made a keening, whimpering kind of sound that seemed too loud to be true. I smiled weakly. "Coincidence," I said. "I had the shrimp for dinner, and I thought it looked a little off. *So...*"

Landon looked down at me, as if in disbelief, and then led me by the arm to the back of the room. We sat down on a long couch in the corner that circled a glossy, black table.

I looked around and raised my eyebrows. "So, *The Red Room.* Why do they call it that? Is all the food red, or something? No white wine? Or maybe you can only order undercooked steaks."

Landon drew my attention to the door. "The red curtain."

"Oh," I said, deflating. "I was kind of hoping Grandpa Willy was more creative than that."

"There are different types of rooms at The Golden Pecker. Private rooms. Public rooms. Passive rooms. *Active* rooms."

I quirked an eyebrow. "Why did you say 'active' all whispery like that?"

"Because I don't think we need to show you the active rooms."

"Because why?"

"It's not on the list, for starters. And I doubt you'll ever be ready to step inside an active room."

"Sorry," I said. "But you keep talking like you know the first thing about me. I'm not some blushing virgin. I've totally done it before. I've even watched porn. So, the idea of somebody getting their hands tied up or spanked with a paddle isn't going to scandalize me into running out of the room screaming."

Landon flashed a rare grin. "You've *done it,* have you?"

I bit back frustration at my choice of words. "I've had sex," I said flatly. "I've *banged.* I even fucked, once. It was all wild, crazy, and wonderful, *thankyouverymuch.*" Truth be told, there was nothing wild, crazy, or wonderful about the sex I'd put on my resume, but Landon didn't need to know that. He definitely didn't need to know that I'd done the deed exactly two times with exactly two partners. The first had been with the man I will forever remember as Speedy McCummins, the potential world record holder for fastest ejaculator on Earth. I could put it this way: if there was a Wild West style shootout where the fastest cummer came out on top, Old Speedy would've knocked them all dead—and he'd have done it with semen in his pants. He also would've been on the bottom, because he had a bad back and couldn't get on top.

My second partner was so bland he hadn't even earned a nickname. I guess if I had to pick something, I could've called him The Little Engine That Could. Emphasis on little. He tried and tried, but the only move in his arsenal was to get sweatier and try harder. I found myself faking an orgasm as a mercy act, after which, he promptly collapsed.

But hey, I really had watched a porno or two, so I wasn't a total liar. And I'd added the coctopus to my reading arsenal, which had to count for something.

"I didn't realize I was dealing with an expert," Landon said. "I apologize. I won't bother explaining what's about to happen then."

I nodded, even though I felt a little pang of fear. What was about to happen that I'd need an explanation to prepare for?

As if in response, the lights dimmed, and a very peculiar group of people walked on stage.

4

LANDON

A topless man in a full mask and leather pants stepped out on the stage. He pulled open a control panel, pressed a button, and waited while a glass screen rose to cut the stage off from the rest of the room. Moments later, blue-lit smoke started to puff out from machines just behind the curtains. Once a haze had fallen over the stage, a table was wheeled out and cranked into an upright position so we could all see the harnesses and straps dangling where the head, hands, hips, and feet would go.

Two more men led a completely nude woman out to the stage, pushing wisps of the blue smoke in their wake as they walked.

I discreetly stole a glance at Andi, who was watching the stage with wide eyes and a tight grip on her legs. I grinned to myself. *Didn't cover this in your pornos, did they?* She looked so deliciously innocent as she sat there. My eyes couldn't help falling to her legs. I chewed my lip, drinking in the hints of her body I could find beneath the conservative clothing.

I thought about my father setting this whole charade up. It pissed me off. I wondered for the first time if he thought his pretend granddaughter was somehow best suited to make a fool of me. Maybe he knew she'd turn down my advances or think she was too good for me.

Well, old man, if that was your plan, you miscalculated.

I let my legs open up wider so that her knee was against my thigh. She twitched, but didn't try to move her leg away. As pathetic as it was, the unspoken permission made a rush of excitement run through me. It was like finding a cracked door in a house that was supposed to be full of locked rooms.

I considered pushing my luck for more, but decided this would all be far more enjoyable if I let it play out slowly. I wanted her dreams to be filled with dark desires. *With me.*

The two men retreated back into the darkness, leaving the woman in front of the table. The masked man approached, and the overhead lighting made each muscle on his body stand out in stark contrast.

He took the woman and methodically tied her to the table. I knew the performers, so I happened to know the masked man was Matt. He was as professional as doms came, and he was careful to secure Crystal to her spot on the table only as tight as he needed. Doms at our club were held to strict standards when they were with their submissives, and we didn't tolerate bruising or cuts.

Every tug of the straps made her large breasts jiggle, and the fact that I was sitting beside Andi while this show was being set up sent an unexpected pulse of excitement through me. I wondered if the thrill I felt was only because I enjoyed giving one last middle finger to William—after all, this was all his idea. Any heartbreak she might come to at my hands would be of his doing.

Then again, I felt a spark with Andi. It wasn't the usual kind of spark, like a dim light in the distance. I felt more awake and alive around her, but I still hadn't figured out if it was because of her, or if it was because she was so closely tied to William . It was enough to make me wonder what I actually cared about. Was I making her do this to screw my old man, or was I just chasing the spark?

Whatever my motivations might be, The Red Room was just an appetizer, and if she kept her nerve, the main courses were going to mean she and I would be spending some time together. I didn't expect that thought to make my dick twitch, but I guess I shouldn't have been shocked. Andi *was* beautiful, after all. She was also the kind of beautiful that seemed to knock my guard down. It wasn't the magazine-perfect type of beauty, either. She didn't have massive, pouting lips and breasts that challenged gravity.

She was real, like she'd somehow managed to thread her way through life in New York City without letting it touch her. I couldn't decide if that was impressive, or if it was a testament to how stubborn and obstinate, she was. I guess it was both.

"What do you think?" I said.

"I'm just wondering if being a nude stage performer in a seedy BDSM club gets you full benefits."

"Why? Thinking about a career change?"

She wiggled her eyebrows. "You wish."

I looked back to the stage. Andi was unbelievable.

Despite her bravado, I could feel how tense Andi was beside me, especially when the performance began in earnest. There was a kind of brutality to watching this sort of show. Life is all about restraint and composure and shame. It's about learning how to hide your desires.

Down here, nobody hid. Crystal bit her lip and watched with half-lidded eyes while the doms set to work on her, running hard, confident hands across her body. She opened her legs for them when they produced a whip and she gasped when they slid the handle inside her.

Andi flinched beside me. I discreetly watched her, noting the way her chest was rising and falling rapidly. After a few moments, I even found a vein on her neck and could see the quick, pulsing pattern of her heartbeat. She was even unconsciously pressing her thighs together.

I grinned to myself. She was aroused. Hell, *so was I*. Except my excitement had nothing to do with what was happening on stage.

I could've put together a very compelling list of good reasons to keep an emotional and physical distance from Andi. Yet none of that seemed to temper the way my thoughts were running in wild, dark directions—filling me with ideas of the things I'd like to do to her.

Half an hour later, Crystal was done moaning on stage and the performers had left.

Some of the crowd had taken advantage of the dim lighting in the seating area to enjoy their partners. One man on the opposite end of the room appeared to be enjoying three women at once, and another was dragging the woman he was with out of the room, probably toward a private area.

Andi turned toward me and gave a little shrug when the performers left the stage. "Meh. That wasn't so bad."

I licked my teeth, then chuckled. "Alright. I'll admit you handled that better than expected."

Andi gave me a wide-eyed, innocent look. "I don't know what you mean."

"I figured you'd make an excuse, run out of here, or maybe even slap me when you saw what was going to happen."

"Oh. I mean, as soon as I saw the shape of the handle of that whip, I was like, 'that's totally going in her ass.' So, it actually was less dirty than I imagined. Come on, right? Whip in the old coocher? That's hardly a scandal." Her eyes flicked across my face, then she flashed a crooked smile. "If I didn't know better, I'd say you're smiling. Or maybe you're constipated... Did you have the shrimp, too?"

"The first one," I said. "And you know, it's almost creepy how much you remind me of your grandfather." She really did, even though there wasn't a drop of blood relating the two of them.

"Like... physically speaking? Or do you mean my personality."

My eyes fell to her chest and the lean shape of her body, which was clad in her aggressively conservative outfit. For what felt like the tenth time that night, I imagined how good it would feel to peel her out of it, layer by layer. "Your personality."

"Anyway," Andi started, "I'm up way past my bedtime. So, as fun as this has been, I'm going to just head back up to an empty room and call it a night." She stood and bobbed off in the completely wrong direction.

In fact, she was heading toward the orgy room. And some legacy members of the club were scheduled for that room tonight. "Uh, Andi," I said, taking a step toward her.

"Nope. I'm not interested in watching any more weird shows tonight. I need to sleep that one off, thank you very much," she called over her shoulder before disappearing around a corner.

I stopped and waited with crossed arms and a smile.

It was a minute later before she returned, walking more stiffly and with much wider eyes. "That was the wrong way." The quiet, stiff tone of her voice made the situation immensely more amusing.

"Why don't you let me walk you out."

Andi nodded, and for the first time since I'd met her, she didn't seem to have much to say.

5

ANDI

Bree paused with the nail polish bottle in one hand and the brush in another. "You're making that up," she said, eyes wide.

I shook my head. "I wish I was." I'd just finished filling her in on the details of last night, concluding with the optical abuse of whatever the hell had been going on in that dark, smelly room. I shuddered at the memory. Until that room, every single man I'd seen had been sculpted and near perfect. *That room.* It had apparently been senior night, and those seniors were all very... *Lively.* It was like stumbling into a room full of humping rabbits in heat, only the rabbits were hairless, wrinkled, and one was loudly asking if anyone had seen its dentures.

Bree leaned in a little. "Are you okay? It looks like you're going to be sick."

"I saw things, Bree. Things no human eyes were meant to see."

"You're exaggerating, though. Right?"

I pointed to my face. "Does this look like the face of somebody who *didn't* walk in on a room full of grandmas and grandpas playing hide the sausage?"

Bree thought about that. "Well, good for them. Just because they're older, it doesn't mean they shouldn't be able to enjoy themselves."

I sighed. "That's not the point. They can have all the fun they want. I just don't want to have to *see* it. Maybe when I'm eighty, I'll have had the time to prepare my brain for something like that."

"You're terrible. I mean, I do hope they were being careful. That sounds like a recipe for somebody to get hurt."

I laughed. "They all looked surprisingly limber, actually. Not that I stuck around long enough to see who could touch their toes and who couldn't."

"And what about Landon?"

"What about him?"

"I mean, didn't the thought cross your mind? This whole situation would be perfect if you wanted to date him."

I laughed. "This isn't exactly the ideal start for a successful relationship. Besides, he..." I shook my head. I was going to say he hated my guts, but that wasn't entirely true. He was *trying* to hate my guts, but I'd seen enough to suspect those feelings were forced. "Just no," I said. "The whole experience was way, *way* too weird. I just need some time to process everything before I go back there. *If*, I go back." Except I knew I was going to. I kept thinking about the way he'd rested his leg against me during the show in the Red Room. It had felt like he was somehow claiming me—*daring* me to move away. But I hadn't. I'd sat there, letting the dirty thrill of it fill me and warm my belly until I had been uncomfortably excited.

Bree squinted. "He's really hot, though. You've at least got to admit that much."

It felt like she'd been reading my mind. I squirmed uncomfortably, then snatched the nail polish from her and started doing my own toes, since she seemed content to sit and talk instead of help. "He also smells weirdly good, and he just looks more and more handsome as the night goes on. But guess what? Landon's looks matter about as much to me as the make and model of a car coming toward me at high speed."

"It's not like that at all."

"And you know because you googly eyed him in the lobby for like, two minutes? Because good looking men couldn't possibly be bad?"

"No," Bree said. "Because an ordinary guy couldn't handle you, I've watched them try. You overpower everybody who tries to get close to you."

"You say that like it's a good thing. But couldn't an argument be made that I should make myself easier to handle?"

"Does a king cobra apologize for being poisonous and terrifying?"

"No..." I said slowly. "Because they are venomous. If them biting *you* makes you sick, they are venomous. If you biting *them* makes you sick, they are poisonous."

Bree waved off my comment. "Nobody cares. I'm just saying it sounds like Landon might be the first guy who can put up with you. Are you really willing to just walk away from that without giving it a shot?"

"I don't know, but why does everybody seem to want to compare me to animals that bite lately?"

"Good question," Bree said. "A better question is what you're going to do about it? Are you going to stop biting, or are you going to keep chomping away until you find a man who can handle a little nibble here and there?"

I laughed. "Seriously. I'm pretty sure I've never bitten anyone in my entire life. But I do get the point you're making. The problem is that just 'handling' me doesn't equate to a guy being a good match. Besides, ever since Landon heard I was a Wainwright, he seemed pretty dead set on hating me."

"And what about before that?"

"You mean the, what, thirty seconds I talked to him in front of the vending machine? He was nicer, yeah. But somehow, I don't think that matters."

"Of course, it does. It means he liked you until he knew who you were. So, all you need to do is show him you're not the person he thinks you are."

"*What?*" I asked.

"Think about it. He started acting different when he heard your last name. In other words, he already had some idea about who you were. He let that idea override what his own eyes were telling him."

"And how would he have a previously held idea about who I am?"

Bree shrugged. "He's a man of mystery. Bonus points."

"None of it matters. I could happily live the rest of my life without that asshole."

"You just said he was nice when you first met."

"Okay? And then he stacked like three hours of asshole on his two seconds of nice." I made a gesture with my hands like I was measuring the two on a scale. No matter what came out of my mouth, I wasn't sure I really believed he was an asshole. I'd seen too many cracks in the mask to really fall for it.

Bree was looking at me in that annoyingly persistent way of hers. "I don't know," she said wistfully. "I've just never seen you talk about a guy like this."

"Like I'm irritated by the idea that he exists?"

"Or like maybe he got under your skin."

I sighed. "What is it you're wanting me to say? I mean, yeah, part of me *wonders* if he and I would hypothetically be a good match in some alternate universe. I've also wondered if a random hot guy in the coffee shop would be a good kisser, but that doesn't mean I went up and tried to make out with him."

"I don't want you to say anything. I just wanted to plant some information in that stubborn head of yours. *You like him, even though you're pretending you don't.*"

My sister was officially delusional. "The part you're forgetting is that *he* doesn't like *me*. My feelings about him are irrelevant. Maybe he's the one you need to be pestering."

"You're just not used to men who aren't intimidated by you. And you're mistaking confidence for disinterest."

"I intimidate people? Since when?"

"You don't care what anyone thinks of you. And you do tend to say inappropriate things at inappropriate times. You also have horrible bathroom etiquette. I've been meaning to mention that."

I set down the nail polish and stood, not caring if I was smearing nail polish on the carpet. *"Bathroom etiquette?* What do you mean, like I forget to say please and thank you before and after taking a dump?"

Bree cringed. "More like the fact that you call it a dump. Or the way you feel the need to... Well..."

"What? Spit it out."

"Sometimes you text me from the bathroom and I know what you're doing in there. It just feels weird."

I laughed. "You're ridiculous. I'm going to start sending you toilet selfies just to see you squirm. How does that sound?"

"It sounds like you need to be tamed. I rest my case."

I threw a pillow at her a little harder than I intended. It connected with her forehead and sent her crashing backwards into the couch. "Yeah," I said in a gritty voice. "Take that like a little bitch."

6

LANDON

I poured steaming tea from the kettle, ignoring how much I hated the smell of the stuff. From the other room, I could hear my mom's hacking coughs. She had started smoking just after the divorce with my dad, and a few weeks ago, we found out her cancer had come back. This would be the third time, and financially, my brother and I were almost completely tapped out from the first two.

Dear old dad had provided some perks to managing his clubs. We both had access to a tailor, and he'd provided us with top of the line clothing to look the part. He'd even given us access to company cars. Beyond what the clients could see, dad didn't care if our stomachs were growling. It was punishment, in his own way. We hadn't chosen him over mom after she cheated, and he never forgave us for it.

My brother, James, leaned against the counter to my side. He had a way of looking like a statue no matter where he was— always preoccupied and always deep in thought.

"She really doesn't know?" he asked suddenly.

"Who, mom?" I asked.

"No. Andi."

I wanted to pretend I didn't know what he was talking about, but I did. I planted my hands on the kitchen counter. "How do you tell somebody something like that?" I asked.

"Plain English?" James suggested in a bored voice.

"By the way," I said in a mocking tone. "Your adoptive grandfather is actually my biological father. See, he got so jealous when my mom cheated on him that he disowned me and my brother. Instead of trying to reconcile things with us, he adopted you and your sisters and became the world's number one fake grandfather. Meanwhile, he treated me and my brother like slaves to further his business interests, barely talking to us except when he had to."

James gave a little shrug. "See? Easy."

I chuckled darkly, then shook my head. "*Fuck.* Sometimes I forget how much I hated him. Just saying it out loud..."

"He was a bastard. *Yeah.*"

Mom coughed again, reminding me to get the tea finished. I dropped in four spoonfuls of sugar, because she liked it sickeningly sweet. My thoughts still raced while I stirred the sugar in. The part I couldn't even bring myself to admit out loud was how I hated that he'd left us nearly destitute. No health insurance. No respectable salary. We had always assumed that there would be some kind of tipping point—some level of success within the club that would mean we'd paid our penance in his mind. That point never came.

He'd also known mom was sick, and he'd *still* let it happen. I was almost certain that part of him knew if he paid us more, we could have afforded better treatment. We could've taken her to the best specialists, gotten her in-home care instead of having to cart her back and forth to hospitals when she was puking her guts up. But the fucking asshole wanted her to die. I know he did.

Mom was sitting up on the couch, looking healthy and beautiful, even still in her late fifties. We hadn't started treatment for this round yet, but she was scheduled to begin soon. I should've been worried about the money it was going to cost, but I knew where I'd get it.

I wondered if dad left me the ability to screw Andi out of her inheritance as one last "fuck you." Maybe forcing her into this arrangement with me was his way of showing me how amazing she was. He knew I'd still do whatever I had to for mom, and he'd chosen Andi to stain my conscience.

I wasn't just going to be stealing from his ghost. *No.* I would've loved that. Instead, I was ripping away *her* inheritance. Cheating her out of it.

"My body may be going to shit," she said in a craggy voice. "But my ears still work. I heard you two talking in there."

I looked down, then set the tea on the table beside her. She had been so young when she met William Wainwright and got pregnant with us. Young enough that I didn't hold what she did against her—not anymore, at least.

"I've always appreciated how you and your brother stood by me. Even when your dad was trying his hardest to get you to cut me out of your lives."

I hated that she still called him dad, but it was too petty a complaint to voice out loud. "I know," I said. More often, these were the kinds of things she talked about. It made me grit my teeth because I knew she was trying to tie up loose ends, like she thought she might not be around much longer to do it.

She looked down, licking her teeth in the same, slow way I always found myself doing when I was thinking hard. "There's no excuse for what I did, but—"

"Mom, you don't need to explain it to me, okay? You're my fucking mom. You brought me into this world, and I'm going to do whatever I can to keep you from getting taken out of it. It's that simple."

She reached out and squeezed my hand. "You're a good man,

no matter how hard you may try to convince everyone otherwise."

I looked away, smiling tightly. *A good man would've told Andi the full truth before letting her start William's list. He also wouldn't blame an orphaned girl for something she had no knowledge or control over.*

I squeezed her hand back but said nothing.

7

ANDI

I had a job writing an advice column for a not-so-popular blogger. She was also a not-so-successful and not-so-wealthy blogger. Unfortunately, she was my friend, and that meant I put up with working out of her studio apartment for an insulting amount of money. I also put up with her ferret, Montague, who would've been put on a sexual predator list years ago if ferrets were held to the same standards as people.

Okay, none of that was entirely true. But the full truth is kind of pathetic, so I've gotten used to burying it. I just wanted to *feel* like my job was writing, even if it meant not getting paid regularly or well.

So day after day, week after payless week, I kept showing up. Not because of loyalty to Rachel or endurance for the sexual exploits of Montague the ferret, but because I wanted to believe this job was a stepping stone. Especially now that grandpa was gone, it felt even more important to be here.

I let myself into Rachel's room because she refused to lock her door, no matter how many times I harassed her about it. The studio apartment was small enough that you couldn't have even practiced a full range of yo-yo moves inside it. The lone window sometimes offered a view of a row of boxes where some homeless people lived on the street below. All in all, it was the kind of perfect charmer that demanded thousands of dollars per month in New York City's housing market.

Rachel was sitting on a pile of her dirty clothes with about seven pens stuck in her hair. She patted around blindly on the nightstand behind her, searching for something.

I plucked a pen from her hair and handed it to her.

"What do you think about sequins? Out of date or coming back?" she asked.

Rachel was probably the most driven and single-minded person I'd ever met. If there was one thing she did well, it was refusing to admit there was *nothing* she actually did well. But to her credit, that never stopped her from busting her ass and using sheer effort to at least do a halfway decent job. In a kind of pathetic way, it was admirable.

Her blog, RachelATM, which was supposed to be short for Rachel's Advice to Mom's, was often visited by horny men who thought Rachel was into ass-to-mouth or that she was ready to print money for them. It was also worth noting that Rachel was not a mom. In fact, she hated kids and never made time to date. As far as I knew, she also wasn't interested in ass-to-mouth and she definitely wasn't printing money.

She was wearing a loose-fitting t-shirt, yoga pants, and thick, red glasses. In the few times I'd seen her around guys, something about her intensity and tight-lipped smiles seemed to scare men away. Still, I thought if she could loosen up long enough to survive a date, there would be plenty of men out there willing to take a shot with her—if for no other reason than the vague prospect of a little ass-to-mouth.

I pulled my laptop out of my bag and sat on the edge of her bed. Rachel tore off a page in her notebook with a few ideas hastily scribbled down for today's advice column.

I raised my eyebrows. "Breastfeeding for dummies?" I asked.

"You have the internet," she said. "Just look it up."

I sighed. "Don't you just kind of stick them on the boob? How hard can it be?"

"Would you just do your job and stop asking questions?"

I glared at her, even though she wasn't looking. "If you want to keep calling it a job, you might consider paying me on the reg."

"If you want more money, try writing a column that actually gets some hits. Then there might *be* some money to give you."

"I keep trying to tell you. Embrace this anal fellatio thing and your site will be a hit. Think of all the unsatisfied men who bounce off the site every day. I can picture it now. 'Ass-To-Mouth: 5 Dirty Tricks.'"

Rachel pantomimed gagging. "How about, Breast feeding: Jug Gotta See These 5 Tricks to Believe 'Em."

I raised my eyebrows. "Jug gotta?"

Rachel held her hands in front of her almost-not-there boobs. "You know. Jugs."

"I got it, I just... Never mind. It's your site!" I said cheerily.

After about ten minutes of looking at pictures of mom's whipping out their milk makers and reading up on the difference between the football hold and the reverse grip upside down cradle style, I was convinced nothing about breastfeeding was appropriate for a dummy. In fact, I was starting to wonder why they didn't offer degree courses at universities across the country on the subject.

Something warm and furry moved between my legs. I jumped back with an annoyed groan. I lifted my laptop to find Montague the ferret pawing at me. I swatted him away, but I knew he'd be back as soon as he thought I forgot. *Little creep.*

I pulled up the word processor on my laptop, but instead of the "Breastfeeding for Dummies," I wrote, "How to Tie Down a Dickweed." I grinned to myself at the thought of tying Landon to a bed and watching the smug confidence slip off his face for once.

Without any clear purpose in mind, I started to write.

The first step to tying down a dickweed is to avoid getting attached. Attachments are weakness, and you will need all of your strength to overcome the dickweed's tendency for manipulation. The dickweed is notorious for using his physical gifts to distract and confuse its prey. But you will not be prey. This time, you will be the hunter. You'll hop on that dickweed and you won't let go until he comes wi-

I paused, re-read the last sentence, then held the delete button for a few seconds.

You'll take control of the situation and won't give it up until you've got your chains tied tight around his wrists. And that's when you walk away, leaving him with a malignant case of blue balls.

I stopped typing when I realized Rachel was breathing over my shoulder. I also noticed her breath smelled like Cheetos. "Who eats Cheetos for breakfast?" I asked.

"Forget that," she said, staring at my computer. "What is this?"

I snapped the laptop shut and scooted away from her. "Nothing."

"Are you seeing someone?"

"What part of any of that made it sound like I was seeing someone? And actually, I gotta go early today. There's some stuff going on with the will I need to look into."

"Hey," she said, frowning as she clearly pondered some deep, troubling idea. "Could you clean up what you were writing and make it kind of like a satire column? You know, like female empowerment meets *Sex and The City* meets *Fifty Shades of Grey*?"

"That's going to be a 'no,'" I said. "If the dickweed in question ever figures out I work for you and gets nosy, I'd die of embarrassment."

"What, if he realizes you're fantasizing about tying him down and his big, blue balls?"

I grinned. "Yes. Something like that. So, forget it."

Rachel chewed the end of her pen. "Think about it. Maybe I'd even pay you on time for something like that."

"When I'm ready to risk the most uncomfortable moment of my life for a big three dollar pay day, I'll let you know."

8

LANDON

Andi left the shabby apartment building around noon. I hopped out of my car and jogged toward her.

I called out to get her attention as I was crossing the street.

She stopped and turned like she was expecting to have to fend off a crazy person. When she saw it was me, her expression hardly changed. I had to admit there was still something about her look I liked. I still couldn't decide if she was innocent and naïve, or if her confident front was real. All I knew was that I'd resorted to stalking her so I could get the truth off my chest before things got any further.

Originally, I'd just planned on telling her when she showed up to the club after my conversation with James. It had been a week since that day at my mom's apartment, and Andi had been like a ghost. Considering I had the authority to go to the lawyers at any minute and call this whole thing off, I thought it was either stupid, brave, or both for her to assume I'd wait around.

I'd lasted a full two days before I made my first weak excuse to wander the lobby of the hotel in search of her. When that proved fruitless, I got more desperate. I even found myself walking the halls of the upper floors on the off chance that I'd cross her path.

I'd like to say my need to find her was purely to unburden myself and explain who I really was. Partly, that was true. But there was another side of me that simply wanted to see her again—to feel that slight rush of electricity I'd felt when I was leading her through the club on my arm.

So, I'd sat outside the hotel in my car and waited to catch her leaving. And I may have sort of followed her to her job. Once I saw the apartment she went to, I was able to do a little detective work on my phone and found the blog she helped with.

Was I neck deep in stalker territory by now? *Yes.* Did I give a shit? *No.*

"What the hell are you doing here?" Andi asked.

"You seem to think this all gets to happen on your schedule," I said. I was beginning to realize I should've planned what I was going to say. I'd been so focused on finding her that I had let the details of the conversation be an afterthought. Now, the same, old anger at my father was creeping in and coloring my words. "Either you finish the list and stop wasting my time, or I'll go to the lawyers. Tonight."

She held her hands up and looked around helplessly. "And you thought stalking me was the best way to get me to come back to your creepy club?"

"No," I said. I still wasn't sure if I was tracking her down because I wanted to use my father's list to break her or if I just wanted more of her. Whatever it was, I knew I needed to do what I'd come here to do first.

I clenched my teeth. *Tell her now. This is the moment where it makes sense. Say that you're William's son, and you let your anger over how he replaced you leak into this whole thing, but now you're ready to be reasonable—to simply hand her the share of his hotel and walk away.* Even as the thoughts skidded around my mind, I knew I wasn't going to take the smart route. I was going to do something stupid, to chase that faint, dark thread of desire I felt for Andi.

The truth seemed to come together all at once in my head.

I didn't care about making her prove she deserved a share of the hotel. I didn't even care about my father's vague promise of some greater reward if I finished the list with Andi. I simply wasn't ready to give her a ticket out of my life. I wanted more. Greedily, I wanted the excuse to keep her tethered to me, even if it was only for the duration of the list. And some small part of me still liked the idea that if this all went to hell, it'd still be a final "fuck you" to my father for being foolish enough to try to force us together.

"Well?" she asked. "Are you going to just growl 'no' and keep staring at me like I'm a turd on your carpet, or are you going to explain why?"

The truth. Tell her the fucking truth, Landon.

"Because I tried my damndest not to like you from the moment I heard your last name. And despite my best efforts, I find myself not hating the idea of spending time with you."

She stared for a few seconds before cocking her head to the side. "Is that like the world's most backward way of saying you like me?"

I found myself chuckling and shaking my head. When I'd planned to tell her the truth, it certainly hadn't been *that* truth. But maybe it was a start. "Let's not get carried away," I said. "All I'm saying is that it's not entirely unpleasant to be around you."

"Jesus," Andi said, laughing. She bit her lip, then smiled. "I can tell you're trying to say something nice, so I'm going to choose to just read between the lines and say *thank you*."

I nodded.

Andi tapped her foot, almost like she was trying to stop from saying what she was about to say. "I'm sorry I disappeared on you. Honestly, I think I got scared. I went into that club to talk sense into you and wound up watching a woman get banged on stage with the handle of a whip. And then there was *you*."

I raised an eyebrow.

She looked up at me with a slightly bashful expression. "I'm just saying it wasn't... horrible. And it's important to me that I finish the list because it's what my grandpa wanted. So, no. I still don't really trust you, but I'm strongly considering moving forward."

I hadn't realized I stepped closer to her, but we were standing very close. Close enough that I could catch the hint of soap on her skin. I felt my nostrils flare as I tried to devour every hint of her fragrance.

"I'm pleased to hear that," I said. The light changed and let a large group of pedestrians cross the street and come toward us. We were pushed even closer together as the crowd of people shuffled by.

Once they were gone, neither of us moved. My hands had naturally found their way to her hips, and I was suddenly aware of how close her lips were—how easily it would be to claim them in mine.

Instead, I took a step back. It felt like bursting a bubble that had surrounded us. As much as I wanted to take everything she had to offer, something was holding me back. Maybe it was not knowing if I only wanted her as some deranged way to get back at my father. Or maybe I just knew how much of a mistake it would be to let things between us solidify when I was still hiding such a huge secret.

"I was planning on going to one of my favorite places this afternoon. I'll take you with me."

"You'll take me with you? Like kidnapping? I think the phrase you're searching for is, 'would you like to join me?'" When I'd stepped back from her, it looked like she had been holding her breath. But she was recovering back to her normal self quickly enough, it seemed.

I gestured. "Sure. That."

Andi sighed. "For the record, I'm not going to serve as your translator from grumpy dick to polite forever. But yes, I'll go with you, as long as you're not under the impression this will be a date, or something."

"You can call it whatever you like. And so can I. *I'm calling it a date.*"

Andi rolled her eyes but smiled.

"So, where does somebody who spends their time in a seedy, underground club called The Golden Pecker go for a date, exactly? Were you going to take me on a tour of Bram Castle to see the inspiration for Dracula? Maybe a museum of torture implements? Oh, even better! We could go to a Hot Topic at the mall, maybe pick out a costume for you to wear tonight."

"None of the above." I said. "But I do like surprises."

Andi looked toward my car, clearly considering her options. I was surprised to find myself anxiously awaiting her response.

She finally let out a long sigh. "You're lucky I love surprises too. And I'm way too curious for my own good. *I'll go.*"

9

ANDI

"An aquarium?" I asked. "I have to admit, this is almost anticlimactic. Like, I was seriously expecting you to pull into some secret cave and tell me you were introducing me to your family. And I thought your family would be a bunch of bats."

Landon ignored me and walked up to the counter while I wandered the gift shop. I stole a glance his way when I saw how long it was taking him to pay. He was leaning forward and talking with the girl at the register in a hushed voice.

A surprising spike of jealousy shot through me. Had he seriously asked me on a date and now he couldn't even make it through the door without flirting?

I tried to casually get closer until I could hear some of what they were saying.

"Yes," the girl said. "Your season pass includes one guest for free. We're not really supposed to..."

"Can she use mine?"

The girl sighed, then smiled. "Forget it. I won't tell anyone if you don't." She grabbed two orange wristbands, scribbled something on them with a marker, and handed them to Landon.

"You're a lifesaver," he said, rapping his knuckles on the counter before heading toward me. When he saw me looking, his face fell.

"What was that about?" I asked.

Landon cleared his throat and grabbed my wrist, wrapping the band around it. "She was just confused about something," he mumbled. The innocent touch of his fingertips on my arm was like electricity. It brought me back to the street and the way he had been so close. I was certain he was about to kiss me, as insane as that would have been, and then it was like that switch in his head had flipped again.

"What is a dolphin encounter, exactly?" I asked.

"You'll love it. Don't worry about it. We've got about an hour to look around before we need to be at the dolphin tanks. They'll explain everything when we get there."

He was still wearing his tailored suit and tie, but I felt like I was seeing him in a different light here. Just a touch of that ominous, *I'd like to eat your face off,* vibe about him had dissipated. If I didn't know better, I'd say he was excited to be here. He should've looked wildly overdressed, but the way he wore his suit so comfortably made him look right at home.

I noticed his tie was off center, just like Grandpa Willy's always managed to become. I instinctively reached out, gave it a little tug, and then patted his lapels once it was straight. Except the face looking down at me wasn't wrinkled, kind, and a little bit goofy. There was only iron and heat in Landon's eyes.

"Force of habit," I mumbled, taking a step back to get me out of his personal space. "Don't go getting a boner about it, weirdo."

He said nothing, but I could feel his eyes on me for a few more seconds before he continued walking toward the first set of tanks in the aquarium.

It was the middle of the day on a weekday, and apparently, that meant the aquarium was almost completely empty. It was also oddly quiet, except for the occasional bubbling gulp of a tank or the hum of pumping equipment.

"It's freezing in here," I said. "You should've warned me to bring a jacket.

Landon slid his suit jacket off and offered it to me. The inside lining was trimmed in a deep, scarlet color. Somewhat grudgingly, I took the jacket from him and draped it over my shoulders. "Thanks," I said. "Jesus, why do you smell like that?" I lifted the arm and gave it another, closer sniff. "If I close my eyes, I can see a shirtless guy in black and white... and he's riding a horse on the beach with a polo stick in his hand—but I don't even know what a polo stick looks like."

Landon frowned. He looked uncharacteristically self-conscious, which I guiltily enjoyed. "Is it bad? I just picked it up from the dry cleaner's this morning, so-"

"No," I said, sniffing again and then shaking my head in irritation. "I just mean what's the point? It's like ice cream tastes and looks good enough as it is. We all know how good it would taste. It doesn't need to try to lure us in even harder by smelling good. It just looks the way it looks and tastes the way it tastes. But imagine if ice cream filled up a room with a smell like cooking bacon, or something. It wouldn't be fair."

"You're saying I smell *too* good? And that you know I'd taste good?"

I realized that was exactly what I'd been saying, even though I hadn't meant to compliment him in the process. "I'm just wondering why you're trying so hard to seduce me. What cologne is this? *Desperation? Aggressive Seduction?* Or maybe-"

"I'm not wearing cologne."

I grabbed his hand and lifted his forearm to my nose, taking a deep sniff. "Oh," I said. "Your skin just smells like that. Of course, it does. Do they scrape off bits of you and distill it to make cologne, or something?"

He let his arm fall to his side and watched me with raised eyebrows.

"Don't look so smug," I said, pushing past him. "I can think you smell good without wanting to jump in your jimmies, okay?"

"Are you capable of making it a full thirty seconds without saying something strange?"

"You looked at the menu, ordered the food, and you want me to apologize because now you decide you don't like it?"

"*What?*" Landon asked with clear exasperation in his voice.

"I am what I am, and you asked me to come here with you. So, either deal with it, or stop complaining."

I expected him to snap back at me, but he said nothing. He just turned his head to look at the fish in front of us.

"What's with the aquarium visit, anyway?" I asked. "This doesn't seem like the kind of place I'd picture you going to."

"And what makes you think you know the first thing about me?" Landon asked. "Because of where I work? Because of my sexual preferences?"

"Yes?"

"And what sort of picture of you would I get using the same criteria? The twenty-something woman who works out of some mysterious apartment building?"

"It's not mysterious," I said. "It's a blog. I write articles for her." I shrugged, feeling suddenly self-conscious. "Granted, it's not a particularly successful one. But some day, I'd like to have my own website, or something."

"Or something?" Landon asked. "Like those books you talked about writing some day?"

"I mean, I'd take writing books. Writing advertising. Journalism, whatever. There's something about taking my personality and injecting it into a thought or idea on the page. I don't know," I laughed a little at myself. "It sounds dumb when I say it out loud."

"Not really," Landon said thoughtfully. "It's your passion. Never apologize for that."

I tucked a hair behind my ear. "And what about you? You act like *my* job is weird. Meanwhile, you're Mr. BDSM. I mean, what's wrong with plain old boinking, anyway?"

"Sex, you mean?"

"Yes," I said. "Sex." I lowered my voice, as if I was worried about the fish hearing us.

"There's nothing wrong with 'plain old' sex. It's just that most people don't understand what BDSM is really about. It's not about some twisted kink or the costumes. It's not even about the spankings or bondage. All of that is just a means to an end."

We passed by giant tanks of deep blue water as we talked, and Landon's attention was split between me and the fish. He'd occasionally stop to rub his fingers over an informational plaque and glance at the words, but never read them—almost as if he already knew what they all said.

"A means to an end... And what end would that be?" I asked.

His expression darkened and he moved closer, raising his hand to touch my cheek. It should have been awkward, but he was so blindingly confident about the whole thing that I just felt mesmerized.

I let him touch his fingers to my face and devour me with his eyes. "Domination and submission. Control." He watched his finger as he ran it in a slow, goose-bump inducing path across my cheek. "There are other ends, but those are the ones I find most interesting."

He turned and looked back at the fish like he hadn't just used some weird BDSM magic to make my whole body turn to jelly. I blinked a few times and tried to regain the ability to think straight. Except every time I started to form a thought, it brought me back to the image of his face just then and the curiosity about what it would be like to kiss a man like Landon.

"Okay," I said. *I needed to talk,* I decided. Standing still and looking at him was just filling my head with bad ideas. Besides, I had to admit my curiosity about this whole BDSM thing was piqued, just slightly. "And what is so desirable about dominating somebody or controlling them? Like, I get why that could be exciting for the one doing the dominating. But who wants to be controlled?"

"I could try to explain it until I'm blue in the face, or I could show you."

My skin prickled with heat. "What, like another one of those demonstrations in The Red Room at The Golden Pecker?"

"No. All you did was watch. You won't understand unless you experience it."

"With you?" I asked. "Is that what this is? Some convoluted scheme to get me to let you spank me on the ass with a ping pong paddle?"

"You said you wanted to proceed with the list, didn't you?"

I studied the look in his eyes. There was a fire there. *A need.* I might still have trouble deciding how I felt about Landon, but there was no denying how my body did.

"I'd want to know exactly what you were planning to do before I officially agreed to anything." My heart was pounding. It felt like jumping without knowing what lay below me.

He nodded. "We can sign a contract, if that makes you feel better."

I laughed, but Landon didn't even crack a smile. "You're serious?"

"It's not all that uncommon. The relationship between a dom and his submissive is a complicated one full of potential pitfalls. It's critical to establish expectations ahead of time."

"So, let me get this straight. The plan is to leave the aquarium and miss the awesome sounding dolphin encounter so you can have me sign a contract explaining what you can and cannot put in my butt?"

"Uh," Landon said slowly. "No. The plan is we finish going

through the aquarium because you haven't even seen the great white shark jaws yet. Then we do the dolphin encounter because it's amazing. *Then* we talk about what I can and can't put up your butt."

I stared back at him.

"That last part was a joke," he said.

I let out a nervous laugh. "Sorry. Usually people smile when they tell jokes. You just kind of had this statue look going on."

He flicked his eyebrows up and shrugged. "Humor has never been my specialty."

"Yeah, no kidding."

We sat across from each other in the aquarium's cafeteria a little while later. A greasy red and white checkered tray of French fries stood between us. Gooey cheese coated the fries like a glorious, golden waterfall of calories. Would we like a side of liquid calories with our crunchy calorie sticks? *Yes, yes, we would.*

I picked one up and ate it, ignoring the way the hot cheese was practically melting my taste buds off.

Landon popped one in his mouth as well. He seemed to forget he was supposed to be a scary jerk for a moment, meeting my eyes and grinning as if to say, *damn that tastes good.* I supposed that wasn't entirely fair. Landon had clearly been trying to be less of a scary jerk ever since he talked to me outside Rachel's. Sure, he wasn't exactly knocking that directive out of the park, but I could tell he was trying.

"How do I know you're not just pretending to be normal?" I asked, narrowing my eyes. "I mean, how hard would it be to act like a normal guy for a few hours?"

"Not hard, I suppose." He picked up another fry, letting some cheese drip off before popping it into his mouth. "But what would I have to gain from tricking you into thinking I'm a halfway decent guy?"

I sighed. "I don't know. But I really don't even know who you are. I mean, how did you even know my grandpa in the first place?"

Landon hadn't taken another bite of the fry he was holding. In fact, his fingers were squishing it so hard now that the potato was seeping out of the crispy exterior. "We were business partners," he said.

"And you got that opportunity because you had a great resume? Which you submitted online at The Golden Pecker's publicly searchable website, right?"

He flashed the shadow of a smile. "No. I knew him prior to getting the job. Our personal connection probably helped me land the opportunity."

"And what personal connection was that?"

"The kind that makes someone feel guilty enough to try to make amends."

I felt like I was trying to pull wet, slippery teeth with my bare fingers. "And what would my grandpa have done to you that would make him feel so guilty?"

Landon focused on the fries again. He was apparently done answering my questions.

I almost pressed him for more details on my grandpa, but I sensed something there. There was an emotional wound in Landon, and it had my grandpa's name written all over it. Asking more questions, no matter how much I thought I might deserve an answer, felt like it'd be the same as rubbing salt on that wound.

"What about that James guy? Who is he?"

"James is my brother. He runs one of the sister clubs of The Golden Pecker. The Diamond Pecker."

"Seriously?" I asked.

He nodded.

"So, you and your brother both manage BDSM clubs for a living. What about your parents? Did they run clubs, too?"

Landon hesitated. "My mom never really made a career for

herself. She tried after..." he paused again, eyes searching for something on the table. "She tried eventually, but by then she was getting too sick."

Another wound. The more I spoke to Landon, the more I understood why he seemed like such a cranky grump all the time. The man's past was riddled with enough scars to make my skin tingle. "And your father?"

Landon's jaw flexed. "He moved on from our family."

"What does that mean?"

"It means he fucked up with us and decided it'd be easier to start over with new people. Lucky for him, it seems like he did a much better job the second time around."

I couldn't imagine all the details that would lead to something like that, but I also felt once again compelled not to dig any deeper. Landon was clearly far outside his comfort zone in answering as many questions as he was. I decided to do the merciful thing and move the topic away from his family.

"So, why BDSM clubs? I mean, how do you even get into something like that to start with?"

"Personal reasons," he said flatly.

I might have normally sighed with annoyance at the dodgy answer, but I instead found myself nodding. I may not have all the details, but I understood one thing about Landon Collins: he had a past that was just as full of tragedy as my own. Everyone had their own ways of coping with tragedy, and I knew that as well as anyone. Suddenly, it was harder to resent Landon for the way he'd acted toward me—not impossible, mind you, but harder.

"And how do you feel about all of this? I mean, I know I wasn't thrilled to learn that my grandpa pretty much told me I had to get sexually involved with a stranger to claim my inheritance. But what about you?"

"Initially? I was irritated. I didn't want to babysit you."

"Initially," I said slowly. "And what about now?"

"Now... I plan to make the best of the situation. You kind of remind me of this turtle. It was in the road, so I stopped to move it out of the way. But the moment I picked it up, it just let out the weirdest, whispery scream. It screamed until I put it down in the grass, and then the moment I turned to go back to my car, it bit my ankle."

I burst out laughing. "That's the dumbest thing I've ever heard. Turtles don't scream."

Landon spread his palms. "This one did."

"Also, I don't bite."

"That's a shame," Landon said.

I really never had been the blushing type, but I felt my face turn hot at his tone. I wasn't the most perceptive girl on the block, but I was pretty sure he was flirting with me. Instead of doing the smooth thing and flirting back, I decided to turn things back to my original question. "Before you compared me to a biting turtle, you said you planned to make the best of this situation. What does that mean, exactly?"

"If you have to sleep in the woods, you might as well kick a few pinecones while you're at it."

I threw my hands up helplessly smiling. "Okay. I'm officially banning you from metaphors. I mean, am I supposed to be the pinecones or the sleeping in the woods?"

Landon actually seemed slightly offended. He took a deep breath and folded his fingers together. "Kicking pinecones is something enjoyable you can do in the woods. I was trying to say I plan to enjoy this arrangement."

I leaned forward. "I just want to make sure I understand. You're saying that Landon Collins, the mysterious BDSM club owner, likes to go into the woods sometimes and kick pinecones for fun? Haven't you ever heard of like... Wood carving? Or burning stuff in the campfire? I mean, kicking pinecones?"

"Enough," he growled. "I get it. You don't think it's fun to kick pinecones. Can we move on?"

I grinned. "I'm just enjoying the image is all. You all dressed in your cute little suit. Maybe you're so excited to get to the woods that you're skipping through a meadow somewhere. Then you see your first pinecone and your face lights up. A big windup, and... *kick!*"

Landon was glaring at me now. "I take it back. The way I feel about this is more like I woke up in the morning to find a bear eating all my food."

I wiggled my eyebrows and then tugged the tray of fries to my side of the table. "Rawr."

10

LANDON

I'd brought a pair of board shorts for myself but had to swing by the gift shop to pick up a swimsuit for Andi.

"You know," Andi said. "I'm capable of picking out my own swimsuit."

She was standing behind me with her arms crossed while I rooted through a rack of matching tops and bottoms. I pulled out a pink suit with white polka dots and put it beside her face. "Yeah. I think this is the one."

She snatched it from me. "If I didn't know better, I'd say you are enjoying the idea of picking this out for me."

"More like the idea of seeing it on you."

Andi smiled, but something seemed to cross her mind that wiped it from her face.

"What?" I asked.

"I'm just trying to figure you out."

I spent most of my life thinking I'd hate you, but I don't. Now I'm too much of a coward to tell you who I really am because I don't want to chase you away. I shrugged. "Is it so out of the ordinary for someone to enjoy your company, Wainwright?"

We walked together to the outdoor area where the dolphin

encounter took place. A few other groups of people gathered to wait with us until we were let into locker rooms to get into our swimsuits.

I found Andi already waiting outside in the pink swimsuit. The body she'd been trying so hard to hide was spectacular. She was athletic, but still with curves in the right places. When she caught me looking, she crossed her hands in front of herself.

"Enjoying the view, perv?"

"Yes." I nodded.

Andi paused, clearly not expecting my answer. "Uh, well, just don't get all excited and mistake me for a pinecone. I'd rather not be kicked today."

"It wasn't kicking that I was thinking about."

"Well, are we going to get to ride some dolphins, or what?" she asked in a slightly high-pitched voice.

We were standing on a patch of blue-painted concrete between three large tanks of water. Each tank had a shallow ledge where customers and trainers could stand in waist level water while the dolphins swam up from the deeper section of the tank.

"Whenever you're ready," I said.

"Back again, Landon?" one of the trainers asked. He was a college-aged kid with oversized teeth and messy hair.

I cleared my throat and tried to glare at him until he got the message. I'd probably been to this thing at least a dozen times in the past year, but I would prefer that bit of information to stay private. Andi already knew too much about me—especially after I was dumb enough to tell her about how much fun I apparently found it to kick pinecones. I wanted to groan at the memory. That had been a massive misunderstanding, but it would've been too awkward to try to clear it up, so now I'd forever be the pinecone kicker in her eyes.

Andi was looking at me funny while a young girl hopped up on a box and started explaining the rules to everyone who was gathered around.

"What?" I murmured.

"Just trying to figure out what your angle is. *Back again*," Andi mused. "It's almost like you're here all the time. And he even remembered your name."

"Back again could also mean I've been here once before. And some people are good with names."

"Sure," she said. "But you also stared at him like you were about to grab a dolphin by the tail and beat him to death with it if he didn't look away."

"Why does your mind jump straight past plausible to ridiculous every single time? Do you even know how much a dolphin weighs? I'd never be able to—" I cleared my throat.

Andi's eyebrows were up. "No, professor. Maybe you could tell me? In fact, I think you could tell me exactly how much a dolphin weighs. You could probably even tell me more about their feeding patterns, couldn't you?"

"What are you implying?" I asked.

"That you're some kind of freaky dork dom hybrid. You waltz around your little club with its golden cock key in your pocket, but deep down, you'd rather be petting dolphins and counting colorful fishes. I saw the way you lit up when that lady offered to tell you more about the clown fish. You looked like a fly who just found an elephant with diarrhea."

I cringed. "A fly who... Where do you come up with these things?"

"Because flies like to eat shit. I just mean you looked really excited."

"Next time, why don't you say that instead?"

"Or maybe I could say you look like you just stumbled on a bunch of pinecones in the forest."

Those damn pinecones.

"You two," the girl standing up on the box called. "Are you listening? What's the number one rule?"

"Listen to our trainers," I said mechanically, then I wished I hadn't. I could feel Andi grinning like an idiot at my side.

"Okay, good," she said. "Moving on!"

"Dork dom," Andi whispered. *"Wisten to our twainers,"* she muttered through stifled laughter.

I briefly considered throwing her into a nearby pool of water. I wondered if she'd look as smug when she was cartwheeling through the air.

WE STEPPED OUT OF THE DOLPHIN TANK ALMOST AN HOUR LATER. I managed to ask our trainer for an extra half hour when Andi wasn't looking. The bonus time meant we got to stay with the dolphins while everyone else headed back to the locker rooms and eventually filtered out, leaving just us, the dolphins, and our trainer. Even Andi had forgotten to be a surly, sarcastic nuisance by the time we were done.

She unbuckled her life jacket with a huge smile on her face. "Okay. I think I'm ready to let it slide that you're weirdly fascinated with coming here. That was amazing."

"Good," I said. "I was really worried about your opinion of me."

My dry tone seemed to bring back the usual Andi. She pursed her lips and crossed her arms, which coincidentally pushed her breasts up in her pink swimsuit. It took a little more effort this time to keep my eyes on hers. The damn woman was seriously starting to tempt me. She practically oozed defiance, and I was getting more and more curious to see how she'd handle a little taste of submission.

"Oh, shit," the trainer said. She tugged on the men's locker room door, which was locked. "I forgot to tell them not to close up, and I don't have the keys for this one. Do you mind hanging out for a while? I've got to track down Kyle for the key to the men's room, and God only knows where he ended up."

"No problem," I said.

"Okay, awesome. I'll send him here as soon as I find him. See you later, right Landon?"

I tried to pretend I hadn't heard that.

"See you later, will she? Do you tie her up at the Golden Pecker, or something?"

"If I didn't know better, I'd say you were jealous."

Andi blew out an unimpressed breath. "You wish."

It shouldn't have mattered if Andi was going to think less of me—to assume I screwed around with any and every woman I met. But for some reason, it did. "She said that because I come here. Kind of often."

The way Andi smiled told me she'd suspected as much. "How often, exactly?"

"At least once a month."

"You are such a dork. I have to admit, though. The dorky side makes you a little easier to swallow. Like slathering a burnt, crusty old French fry in a few gallons of ketchup. The dolphin thing is the ketchup, and you're the old, nasty French fry, by the way."

"Yeah. I got that much. I also got that you're planning on swallowing. It's good to get this kind of information out in the open." I was teasing her, but only because if I didn't, I worried I'd open up —that I'd start blabbing about what this place meant to me and why I came so much. Or worse, that I'd talk about my parents—about how things were before the divorce and before my brother and I were replaced with Andi and her sisters.

Andi glared, then pointed to the locker room. "Your clothes aren't even in there," she said. "So, you can wait out here while I go get changed."

"Or," I said. "We could cross an item off William's list. You'd be that much closer to getting me out of your hair."

She lifted her big, doe eyes to mine, and I was completely taken off guard by how fucking hot her hesitation made me. I'd expected cold refusal. Instead, I saw a battle waging behind those eyes.

"Which item, exactly?" she asked slowly. "Because I don't remember anything on the list about you watching me change clothes."

"Bondage."

She laughed, then took a step back. "That sounds like a horrible idea." She shook her head more firmly, as if she was convincing herself now. "Very bad idea."

"I thought you wanted to finish the list."

"I do. But here? I was thinking at the club or something."

I should have given it up. The truth was I'd be able to take things much further in my element. Here, I'd need to show much more restraint. But I'd been walking a thin line for what felt like hours. I had almost taken the kiss I wanted. *Almost.* I knew I needed something, or I was going to lose my damn mind. "What if I promise I won't lay a finger on you?"

She paused. "So, you'd just tie me up and... what, stand there?"

"Something like that," I said with a casual shrug.

"And I can keep my clothes on?"

"Your swimsuit will work. But it won't count if you get dressed again."

She gave me a skeptical look. "I don't remember hearing Grandpa Willy say anything about a dress code."

"There's a reason he entrusted me to see you through this list. I understand the purpose of each item on the list, and as your—" I had to stop myself. I was about to say, "as your dom." I was not Andi's dom. I wasn't even her friend. I was her... *Shit.* I didn't even know what to call this. I was the executor of her grandfather's will, and I was entrusted with giving her a taste of BDSM. "As the person William trusted to do this, I'm obligated to make sure it gets done right."

She looked up, sighed, and then fixed her eyes back on mine.

"Fine. You've already had plenty of chances to ogle me in my swimsuit as it is, I guess."

I pushed open the door to the locker room and gestured. "After you."

Andi slowly walked past me, and even after an hour in the saltwater, I could still pick up a hint of her shampoo. I couldn't be sure if it was intentional, but her hip grazed against me as she walked in. The innocent contact felt like yet another tease—another subtle invitation for more that I knew I shouldn't take.

When I turned to follow her, my gaze fell to her ass, which was practically begging for the palm of my hand. She looked over her shoulder and caught me looking. "You know," she said, turning to back pedal toward her locker. "The more time I spend around you, the surer I am that you're just trying to get into my pants."

"I've never understood that phrase." I kept walking until she was forced to back into the locker. Her breath caught when I stopped advancing just inches from her, forcing her to tilt her chin up to look into my eyes. "It'd be a pretty strange fetish to want to be inside your pants. Especially considering your pants are in here," I said, tapping the locker. "Most men would probably be more interested in what's right in front of them."

"A pair of healthy knees ready to slam into their balls?" she suggested.

I chuckled. "I've been wanting to see what you look like with a little of your bite taken away ever since your first smart-ass comment. Give me your hands."

She hesitated just long enough to remind me that she was still stubborn but stuck her wrists out.

I paused. "Actually, I'm going to need your top, unless you see something else that I could use to tie your hands."

She lowered her hands to plant them on her hips. "Nice try, but I think this will do." Andi pulled at the waistband of my board shorts and tugged on the drawstring, undoing the knot. I watched, oddly fascinated to see her hands working at my waist-band. I wondered if she noticed that her tugging was pulling the fabric away from my body enough that she could've had an eyeful if she wanted. She had to have seen I was already hard. My dick was pressing against the board shorts just inches from her hand, and just as she was finishing up, her finger brushed against it.

I heard her suck in a quiet breath, but she kept her eyes down.

I grinned, plucking the string from her fingertips. "This will do," I said.

I tied a careful knot around her wrists—one that wouldn't tighten itself if she struggled. I made sure it was snug enough to keep her from sliding her hands free, but not so tight that it'd leave a mark. Then I hooked the other end of it through the grate in the locker behind her and tied that off as well.

I took a step back to admire my work. Andi was watching me with an unimpressed look on her face and both arms over her head. Her top was also getting pulled up enough that I could see just the faintest hint of her pale breasts sticking out from the bottom.

"Wow," she said sarcastically. "This is life changing. Now I don't have to wonder what it's like when you get a wedgie and can't fix it."

I looked around the locker room and found a thin towel. I grabbed it, then walked back toward her. "Stay still," I commanded. I carefully tied the towel around her eyes.

"Bondage is about more than simply being tied up," I said. I greedily admired her as she stood there on display for me, arms outstretched and chest rising and falling. She had perfectly smooth legs with just the right amount of tone. "It's about learning to embrace submission."

"I'm not exactly the submissive type," Andi said. "Frankly, I think history is full of women who should've been kicking more men in the balls and speaking up. Being a submissive just feels like an insult to their memory. Besides, I'm—"

"Stop talking and listen," I said. I let my voice be just firm enough to cut her off and remind her of her position. "This isn't submitting in some sort of political sense." I ran my eyes down her stomach, lingering on her belly button, which was stretched into a thin, vertical line. "It's about power. It's about learning that it takes more strength to let go than it does to grab control."

"False. Have you ever seen Cliffhanger? Pretty sure any weakling could let go and—"

"Enough," I snapped. I wasn't sure if I should laugh or groan in frustration. Was there really no point where Andi would start taking this seriously? I leaned in close and lowered my voice to a whisper. "Let go," I said. "Give your trust to me, and I'll give you an experience you could never imagine."

"I have a pretty good imagination," she whispered back with a playful edge to her voice.

Despite my obviously growing interest in the woman, I had planned to keep this encounter relatively tame. But her complete refusal to be serious was driving me to my limits.

"You think this is a joke, don't you?" I asked.

"No. I mean, I've got a towel over my head and my hands are tied together by your swimsuit drawstring. I'd say things are highly serious right now."

"Then there'd be no danger in letting me stretch the rules?"

"Uh, how so?" she asked slowly.

"I won't lay a finger on you, but I'll come close."

She paused for a long time. "You know what? Go ahead. I once sat through a magic act at a school talent show where none of the kids' tricks worked. I can survive awkward and uncomfortable. So if you want to try to prove to me that this is supposed to be some kind of surreal *experience*, go right ahead."

I stared in slight disbelief. I wondered if she knew how many of my buttons she was pressing, or how badly she was making me want to see her come. I don't think I'd ever wanted to make someone climax purely out of spite before, but she had brought me to that point.

I put my lips just an inch from her neck and let out a slow, hot breath.

"Oh, thanks," she said casually. "It's pretty cold in here. Do you mind hitting my arm pits, too? They're kind of exposed."

I was going to make her regret pushing me to this point.

11

ANDI

His hot breath moved from my neck to my chest, then on the top of my cleavage. I tried not to gasp and mostly failed.

There were two camps at war in my brain at the moment.

One camp was the jaded, annoyed section. All the thoughts on that side of my head were about how ridiculously silly this all was. That part of me wanted to roll my eyes at all of this and let Landon get knocked down a peg. He wasn't some master seducer or self-proclaimed "dom." He was just a ridiculously hot guy who liked to play with leather toys, kick pinecones, and look at dolphins.

But the other camp... It was gradually gaining ground and threatening a full-mind-takeover any minute. That side of my brain was painfully, *excruciatingly* aware that the most attractive man I'd ever seen was currently playing breath hockey with my half naked body—that I was tied to a locker in my swimsuit while a Greek God was trying to turn me on out of frustration.

The only thing both camps could agree on was that the more I pissed him off, the more desperate he got to pleasure me. The stubborn part of me liked the idea of him trying and failing. The other part was fully ready to sink into his silly little game and do whatever it took.

I flinched when he suddenly blew out almost cold air against my breast. It was cold enough that I felt it trickle through my top and make my already hardening nipples rock hard. I was highly confused for a second on how he had the mysterious power to change the temperature of air coming out of his mouth, but then I realized he must have just been compressing his lips.

It wasn't just hot, it was thrilling. I was tied up tightly enough that I knew the only way I was getting out of this situation was chewing off my own arms or if Landon let me out. Whether I liked it or not, I was at his mercy. Maybe that could've made me feel objectified or violated, but it made me feel more like a prize —like the kind of sexy, man slaying vixen I absolutely was not.

When he started to kneel and breathe his way down my stomach, I could see a glimpse of him from under my towel, as long as I tilted my head back and looked straight down.

I wasn't ready for the sight of Landon kneeling with his mouth hovering just millimeters from my skin on its slow path down to my belly button and below. I definitely wasn't ready to see how much he appeared to be enjoying himself, *or* the clear bulge pressing against his board shorts.

Was he going to actually do his little blowing act between my legs? And would I be able to resist ruining the moment by thanking him for the blow job? These were all highly important, desperate questions running through my head.

All those questions evaporated as soon as I felt the puff of warmth on my inner thighs. With a single breath of air, all the good sense and logic were blasted out of my system. All that was left was the overpowering urge to throw my legs around his neck and bury his face between my—

Get a hold of yourself, Andi. Sure, I'd apparently made a slight miscalculation by letting myself get into this situation to begin with, but that didn't mean I had to let him win. All I had to do was ask him to stop. Politely, kindly insist that he untie me, and stop making my whole body hum with that gorgeous sense of white hot bliss he was blowing between my legs.

I laid my head back against the lockers, bit my lip, and wrapped my fingers around the string holding my hands together. In a few minutes, I was definitely going to give him a piece of my mind. *Just a few more minutes.*

The door to the locker room opened. "I couldn't find anyone waiting outside, so I've got my hand over my eyes if anyone is in here," a guy called out. "The men's room is unlocked. So, uh, when you guys are done doing... *that. Yeah,*" he added, then the door closed again.

My heart was pounding even harder at the thought of someone walking in on us. It also cemented that this was, in fact, real.

I'd been hovering in this zone of disbelief, and the sound of that door had snapped me out of the haze in an instant.

"Did we just get caught?" I asked.

"Yes." Landon said. "Sort of. But that doesn't mean we have to stop."

I didn't want to stop, but I needed to. Any longer, and I wouldn't be able to stop. I'd be his, and I knew it. "Actually, I really need to pee," I said. It wasn't entirely a lie. I'd sipped down a mega sized cup of Diet Coke while we were waiting to be let into the dolphin area, and my not-so-mega sized bladder was about to throw in the towel. I did a little headbanging motion until the towel fell from my face, giving me a tantalizing look at Landon, who was still on his knees with his face right *there.*

"You need to pee?" he asked.

"Yes?"

Landon gave me a dry look. "It's fine," he said, standing and reaching to untie the knots holding my hands together. "The goosebumps on your skin told me all I needed to know. That, and the way you were trying to press your hips into my face."

"If that's what you want to think," I said. "Or maybe I just enjoyed the thought of relieving myself on your head."

"Interested in urine play. *Noted*," he said clinically. Then he took my wrists and turned them over. He ran his thumb across the slight indentation from where I'd been leaning into the ropes. "These shouldn't bruise," he said absently. "You have very delicate skin, though. You may want to apply some lotion when you get home."

He caught me giving him a puzzled look, then shrugged a little. "Part of being a good dom is leaving no mark," he said.

"Got it, Buffalo Bill. It will put the lotion on its skin when it gets home. So, what happens next?" I asked.

"You come back to the club and we keep moving through the list, or I get your share of the hotel."

I was immediately reminded of why I definitely shouldn't have enjoyed his little "blow job." In an indirect way, I was trying to ask if everything that happened here meant we were some kind of item. Like a couple, even. I felt too silly to say it out loud, though. Apparently, Landon wasn't wondering the same thing. "It doesn't bother you at all?"

"What?" he asked.

"Trying to seduce me one minute and then practically blackmailing me the next?"

Something passed across his face. *Sadness? Hesitation?* Whatever it was, it was gone as quickly as it came.

He let out a chuckle that didn't sound entirely genuine. "No. I don't feel bothered about reminding you why we're both here. You're here for your grandfather, and I'm—"

He trailed off, looking suddenly uncomfortable.

"You're what?" I prompted.

"Trying to do the right thing," he said.

"So today was just an act?"

"No," he said with a sigh. "For some reason, I seem to enjoy spending time with you."

I smiled. "See? That wasn't so hard, was it?"

"No. But I'm not the only one who has trouble admitting the truth."

I tilted my head. "What is that supposed to mean?"

"You and I both know you are excited about finishing the list with me. But you're trying very hard to pretend you're not."

"Speculation," I said, as if I was in the middle of a courtroom drama. The issue was that the prosecutors probably could've pulled out plenty of damning evidence to support his claim—especially if they had access to my brain.

"If you say so. When can I expect to see you again?"

"I'm going to go get a good, healthy dose of normal. And then, *maybe* I'll consider moving on to item number three on the list. And just so your already big head doesn't get any bigger. I want to be crystal clear about something. I'm willing to have fun where I can in all of this, but I still don't trust you. In fact, I'm pretty sure you'd find some way to break my heart and suck the life out of it if I ever did."

"Wow. Anything else?" he asked.

"Yeah, do you know how to open these stupid combination locks? I can never do it right."

Landon asked for my combination, and then opened the locker. "A lacy pink thong?" he said, lifting it out of the pile of my balled-up clothes. "Was this for me?"

I snatched it out of his hands. "It was for the dream guy I hoped would come in and sweep me out of this nightmare."

Landon grinned wickedly at that and leaned closer. "I could get used to being your nightmare."

Something about his tone made my belly fill with heat.

Once again, I thought he was going to kiss me. *No.* The look he was giving me was more like he was about to strip me bare and devour every inch of me. I shuddered at the thought, and not because it was unpleasant. All I would need to do is lean in, to reach up and pull his face down to mine. I could *feel* it so strongly

I knew it was true. He was just waiting for permission—permission to *take* me.

It didn't help that he was still topless from our dolphin encounter, or that I'd barely been able to tear my eyes off the way his muscles corded and flexed with every movement. Every inch of his body was so full of power that I knew he could hold me down and keep me right where he wanted without even straining.

God. Why did that thought make it feel like glitter was trickling across my skin.

I took a shuddering breath. Not yet. Landon was hiding something from me. I knew that much, and I also knew that almost everything good that had ever entered my life had either wound up buried and dead, or gone up in flames.

Trust wasn't something you gave away without serious, *serious* thought. And I trusted Landon enough to keep participating in this little dance of ours, but not enough for more.

"My nightmare?" I said, inching backwards to give myself more space to breathe—space that wasn't occupied by him and that ungodly good smell of his. "Well, don't look so pleased with yourself. I always have nightmares about really nasty public restrooms. So you can try to sound all sexy if you want, but, *yeah.*"

Landon straightened, but still looked like his mind was racing with dark, *dark* ideas. "If I don't see you soon, I'll come find you. William's orders," he added, as if it was an afterthought.

I grabbed the rest of my clothes, thought about saying one more smartass comment, and then decided it was better to just leave. Landon had a way of turning my sarcasm and attempts at humor into twisted sexual perversions. Worse, it felt like the more I resisted him, the more I could see some kind of growing, ravenous desire for me welling up inside him.

12

LANDON

I ran my finger across the golden rooster emblem that was engraved into the bar. Once again, Andi was keeping me waiting. Instead of doing the self-respecting thing and moving on, I'd barely been able to think about anything else. It had been nearly a week since I tied her up and got my first taste. I'd been dead sure she would come crawling into the club after that, maybe even that same night. She could lie to my face if she wanted, but I'd seen the way she reacted to the promise of my touch. I knew how badly she craved it.

But when a day turned into days, and now days were threatening to turn into a week, I was forced to wonder if I'd read her wrong.

James turned his head and took me in with those dark, penetrating eyes of his. The question on his face was clear.

"She'll come," I said, almost to myself.

"What makes this one different?" he asked in his deep, gravelly voice.

He might not have said as much, but I knew exactly what he meant. *What makes her different than Sydney?* Sydney had been like the finale in a long, frustrating string of relationships. I'd vented to James afterwards about how I was done for the foreseeable future. No more dating. Women were just out to use me in one way or another, and I'd sworn I wouldn't fall into that trap again.

"She's different," I said. *Was she?* After all, Andi had a very obvious reason to continue pursuing me. I held her inheritance in the palm of my hand. If she pissed me off, she probably knew it was likely to cost her everything.

James' gaze seemed to shoot straight through me.

I sighed. "Alright. Fine. I don't know if she is different, but I hope she is. I've enjoyed spending time with her, and I'm willing to put myself on the line again."

"Fair enough," James said in his rumbling voice. "Speaking of mistakes." He lifted his glass and tipped it toward something behind me.

I followed his eyes and tensed. Sydney was standing on the other side of the lobby. She was wearing a sheer dress that left nothing to the imagination. She was sleek with almost exaggerated proportions.

She made a point of noticing who was admiring her, so it only took a few heartbeats before she caught me looking. She smiled in a self-satisfied way and started toward my brother and me.

James didn't waste any time. "Count me out," he grumbled, standing and leaving without hesitation.

Bastard.

Sydney eyed him over her shoulder and then turned her attention to me. She had silky black hair and the eyes of a seductress. None of that had any effect on me. Not anymore, at least. She had been like an island oasis in a long, lonely stretch of ocean once. I'd learned the hard way that those waters weren't nearly as beautiful as they seemed—that just beneath the waves were razor sharp rocks and coral that would have torn me to shreds if I hadn't left when I did.

In a way, I probably should've thanked her. She had been

enough of a nightmare to finally snap me out of it. I hadn't dated a woman like her since she and I broke up. Hell, I hadn't dated, period.

"Sydney," I said coldly. "I thought you were spending your time at The Diamond Pecker, lately."

"Maybe I missed you," she said with a teasing edge to her voice. "I heard a little rumor that you were courting a new submissive."

"That's interesting," I said.

"But is it true?"

"It's not your business anymore."

She titled her nose up, just slightly. Sydney was the daughter of a real estate mogul, and she'd been raised to believe anything she wanted should be hers—information and people included. "You're not still sour about how things ended between us, are you?"

I gritted my teeth. "If I lost a piece of gold, I would be upset. But if I found out that piece of gold was fake, why would I care anymore?"

She sniffed dismissively. "It's cute when you try to hurt me. You want everybody to think you're some tough, imposing dom. But I know how soft you are on the inside. I know all about what your daddy—"

I stood suddenly. The screech of my chair cut her off mid-sentence. "We're done," I growled. The coward inside me quickly put it together. If Sydney so much as suspected that Andi didn't know the truth about who my father was, she could ruin everything.

"Landon," she purred in an attempt to placate me. She reached to toy with the lapels of my jacket. "You trusted me enough to open up to me once. Just because we broke up, it doesn't mean you can't talk to me anymore."

I removed her hands. "We're done," I repeated.

"I'll be here when you change your mind, sweetie," she called after me. "And say hi to that new submissive for me. I can't wait until I have a chance to tell her all about you."

I tensed, and I nearly turned to warn her to stay the hell away from Andi. I knew Sydney, though, and that meant giving her any sign of how much she'd gotten under my skin would only encourage her. It might also tip her off to the fact that I was hiding a dangerous truth from Andi. With an effort, I kept walking.

One thing was certain. Sydney wasn't the sort of problem that went away if you ignored it long enough. Now that she had her sights on screwing up whatever was or wasn't building between Andi and I, it was only a matter of time before she got involved.

I HEADED UP THROUGH THE WINE CELLAR AND INTO THE HOTEL proper. I cut through the lobby, down the West Wing of the hotel, and descended the stairs to the indoor pool below the first level. I found a locker and changed into a swimsuit.

Sometimes, all I wanted to do was float and let my mind clear. Today, I felt like I needed to burn off some frustration, so I was going to get in a workout.

The familiar smell of chlorine filled the echoey room. An elderly man was swimming laps in one of the lanes, but I otherwise had the pool to myself. I dove in and started to stroke in a measured but aggressive pace. There was a point of exhaustion where I'd be too tired to think—too tired to let my mind pick through Sydney's words and the memories they stirred up. It'd also mean I could stop worrying about whether Andi would ever come back to finish the list. That point was my goal. I just wanted those few minutes of blindness.

I reached the other end of the pool, reversed, and kicked off the wall. I broke the surface again and kept stroking, but faster this time. Unwelcome memories bubbled up. I saw my father when he'd still preferred getting drunk every night to spending time with us. I saw the look he'd always get on his face before he'd lose his temper. I saw mom crying after everything fell apart. I closed my eyes and pushed harder, even though it felt like my lungs were beginning to burn.

After a few more laps at a near-sprint pace, I had to stop and gasp for breath with my arms on the edge of the pool.

"You okay?" asked a girl I vaguely recognized.

I pulled my goggles off and then remembered where'd I'd seen her. She was Andi's younger sister, Bree.

"Not sure your sister would approve of you talking to me," I said.

Bree gave me a mischievous, crooked smile that reminded me of her sister. She sat down cross legged by the edge of the pool. She was dressed like she'd just finished exercising in leggings and a bright blue, sleeveless top. I could see a lot of Andi in her, but she didn't have the same aggressively sarcastic and difficult vibe about her. Instead, I thought she was probably the type of girl teachers loved and parents dreamed about having. A good person. "Andi isn't my mom," she said. "So, I don't need her approval."

I laughed. "And you're lucky for that."

Bree smiled. "Okay, to be fair, Andi and Audria actually did practically raise me. So, she's not technically my mom, but I'm also kind of terrified by the idea of pissing her off. So... please don't tell her I talked to you."

"Yeah. I can see how Andi would inspire terror."

Bree's eyebrows drew together. "Have you seen her again? She told me about the whole club thing, but that was it."

Something in my tone must've given away that I knew her better than a single night together could've explained. Bree was perceptive, it seemed. "If your sister didn't want to talk about it, I don't think it's my place to say."

Bree nodded. Apparently, she was also respectful of her sister's privacy. "I actually wanted to find you because I was curious. Did grandpa say anything to you about a video for Audria and I? It's just that it has been a while now since Andi got hers, and since you knew about that one—"

"Nothing, sorry."

"Right. I just thought it'd be worth asking." Bree started to get up.

"Hey," I said, hating that I was desperate enough to ask what I was about to ask. "Is Andi okay? I haven't heard from her since—" I cleared my throat. "It's been a while."

Bree smiled knowingly, then sat back down. "Why do you ask?"

"The smile on your face says you know exactly why I'm asking. Do I have to say it?"

She shrugged. "Sometimes it's nice to have your suspicions confirmed out loud."

"Fine. I'm asking because I wasn't ready to be done with the Andi chapter of my life."

"Wow," she said. "That's a lot more emphatic than if you'd just said, 'yeah, I like her.'" Bree stroked her chin. "The Andi *chapter* of your life. Hmm."

"Well?" I asked. "Is she okay?"

"Oh, she's fine. She has just been going to work and mysteriously avoiding the lobby of the hotel. But now I guess I know why that is."

"She's avoiding me?"

"You know," Bree said. "I know I'm young, and this is probably going to make you want to roll your eyes. But I've always been good at reading people. Andi, she's a lot more delicate than she lets on. All the jokes and sarcasm are just like her walls. Relationships have never really worked out for her, so maybe she's too scared to try again."

"I see," I said. "So tracking her down and pushing the issue might just push her farther away?"

Bree thought about that. "I'm not sure, but I have a feeling if you wait long enough, she'll find you."

"What makes you so sure?"

Bree shrugged. "Like I said, I've always been good at reading people. That's just what my gut tells me."

"Comforting," I said. I slid my goggles back on over my eyes. "Any last nuggets of wisdom?"

"You're arching your back too much. Try to keep your core a little tighter on those front strokes."

I squinted at her.

"Swim team for four years," she said. "You could be really good, you know, if you had a hint of form. And if you weren't an old geezer," she added with a grin.

"I'm thirty-four," I said dryly.

"Yeah, nearly double my age. See ya, geezer," she said, standing and walking off.

I shook my head. Maybe my judgment of Bree hadn't been entirely accurate. She had some of that patented Andi obnoxiousness lurking in her, as well.

I started swimming, but no amount of exhaustion could push Andi from my thoughts.

One night in the club together. One date. That had been all it took to plant a seed that seemed to want to grow out of control. The way she kept vanishing out of my life only made it worse.

I wasn't sure I could follow Bree's advice of leaving Andi alone for any longer than I already had, but I knew I had to try.

13

ANDI

I pulled up the neckline of my dress, only to have it fall right back down into its revealing position a moment later. I was just outside the wine cellar entrance to The Golden Pecker.

It had been exactly one week since our little dolphin extravaganza at the aquarium. My plan had been simple. *Cool off.*

There was no point denying it. My experience with Landon had been hot. Like, microwave hot—the kind of hot you could only get by accidentally adding a zero when microwaving a potato and you leave it in for twenty minutes instead of two. There was only one thing to do in those situations. You step back from the potato that is glowing like the core of an angry, dying sun, and *wait.* Even when you think it might be safe to touch, you still don't.

Except I had unfortunately learned that my potato was still in the microwave. Waiting had only intensified everything I felt. All the confusing desires and the curiosity and even the grudging admission that I was starting to like Landon. No, I'd liked him from the first encounter. I was starting to *crave* Landon, and that was a much, much more dangerous proposition.

Tonight, I was going to put an end to it. Waiting was only

making me crazier. If my goal was not to get emotionally tied up with a man, I was sure would eventually break my heart, I needed to get this over with.

So there I was, dressed a little more to fit in at The Golden Pecker, but still mostly within my comfort zone.

I'd texted Landon and asked him to let me in. I could've used Audria's dildo again, but that would've involved asking my sister to borrow her dildo. For obvious reasons, I went with the more direct approach. It was the most straight-to-the-point, I'm-definitely-not-into-you text I could think of: "Let me in, asshole."

His reply of "K" came a few minutes later.

I wasn't exactly expecting him to send a gushing, grateful text that I'd finally stopped blowing him off, but still. The bastard could've at least typed the whole word out.

I leaned against the door and tried to look bored, annoyed, and casual all at the same time. I even ran over some biting things I could say when he showed up. *Let's get this over with, dickface.* Or maybe... *Yes.* I grinned to myself. I had the perfect idea.

There was a faint clicking noise from behind me, and then the wall I was leaning on fell away.

I pinwheeled my arms for a few seconds and then wound up plopping on my ass, which was currently clad in a shortish dress that was much less conservative than what I wore my first night.

Landon hooked me under the arms and lifted me to my feet as if I weighed about as much as a loose booger—not that I knew how much boogers weighed, for the record.

I dusted myself off. "Thanks, but I can stand up on my own."

"I'm glad you came back," he said. "I have to admit, I—"

I held up my palm to stop him. All the distant fear I'd felt about my growing feelings for Landon seemed to double in an instant. I was afraid he'd say something that was going to make me fall deeper, so I did what I always did—something stupid. "Actually. I didn't come here tonight for Grandpa Willy's list. *Or you.* I wanted to experience the club for myself a little bit." Of course, it was a bold-faced lie, but I couldn't seem to help myself from sabotaging whatever feelings he might have for me.

"That's not a good idea," Landon said. The way his dark hair was slightly messy and coming loose over his intense eyes had an admittedly startling effect, but I refused to be swayed.

"Thankfully I'm not obligated to live according to what you consider a good or bad idea. So..." I weaved around him and started walking down the hallway toward the lobby of The Golden Pecker.

Landon caught me by the shoulder and turned me to face him, almost roughly. The suddenness of it pissed me off, and I shoved him by the chest. Hard. Except he was too solid to be moved, so I only succeeded in hurting my wrists and nearly falling backwards.

I saw anger, rage, and maybe even a flame of desire explode in his features as he advanced toward me. As much as I wanted to hold my ground, I couldn't help being backed toward the wall. He slapped one palm against the wall above my head and bent down. His lips crashed into mine, pushing my head back with the force of it.

All I did was survive the moment for the first few seconds— like being caught in a massive wave so big the only option was to relax and hope you weren't dashed against the jagged rocks just below the surface.

Then I was kissing him back. My emotions were a tangled ball I didn't even care to try to decipher. All I needed was the press of his lips against mine—that velvety crush of warmth that made it feel like my world had turned to glitter and fireworks.

His hands were so big and possessive, pulling me in, clutching me to his body as if he was afraid I might go somewhere.

I pulled back instinctively. It couldn't have been more than ten seconds, maybe less. But my heart was pounding and I couldn't seem to catch my breath. Every nerve in my body was lit up like the Fourth of July, and Landon was staring down at me like he was just as shocked as I was.

"No," I said. "You don't get to do that—to just," I pushed him back and moved away, waving my hand angrily. "You're hiding something. I know you are. And if you think being an amazing kisser is going to make me forget about it?" I laughed mirthlessly.

I really didn't know what I wanted. I just knew I was angry. Angry that my grandpa couldn't just pass away and let me handle the grief of losing him. He had to put this cruel twist to it all and send me on the most emotionally confusing journey of my life. And then Landon had to constantly tempt me with the promise that he might be some perfect guy, even though he was obviously keeping something from me.

"You're right, I'm sorry." Landon said. His words came out clipped and controlled, like he was trying hard not to say more.

"I'm right. You're sorry? That's it? You could try telling me what it is you're hiding. What's the big secret? Huh? Or were you hoping you could just let me fall for you so deep that I'd forgive you for being a liar?"

"It's not that simple."

"It's pretty damn simple. There's the truth, and then there's you. Truth, meet a stranger named Landon. I know you two haven't met before, but he would love to give you a try."

"Andi..." Landon said.

"No." I held up my palm and shook my head. "I'm going to check out the club for myself. Or will going in there reveal your secret? Is that why you're trying so hard to stop me?"

"It's not safe in there. For you."

"I can take care of myself."

"I'm aware. Trust me," he added, almost reluctantly. "But it's a different world in there. There are rules you don't know about. Customs you'd be walking blind into. Somebody could misinterpret, they could think..."

"What? Spell it out for me, Landon. They'll think I'm free

game? That I want to *fuck*? And what if that's all true? Is that a problem for the executor of my grandfather's will? Because I find it hard to believe you hang out in here every night and don't go exploring on your own. So is it just me that isn't supposed to have any fun? That's what you want me to be, right? Something you can put in a display case and play with when it suits you?"

Inside that head of his, Landon was clearly at war. There was something he was trying desperately to say—or maybe not to say. "This isn't about what I want. Letting you go in there by yourself, looking like that... You don't understand what you'd be doing."

"Looking like what?" I asked, even though I hated how much I knew what I wanted his response to be.

"You look exactly like the kind of pure, pretty little thing a seasoned dom would love to claim. Some doms would happily take you, manipulate you, and turn you into their plaything before you knew what happened. Not all of them would, but some are predators."

My eyes narrowed. "And tell me, how is that different from the way you tied me up and seemed to want me to enjoy it so badly? Why should I believe you're not one of those predators?"

"Right," I said, sliding out from under his arm. "If you're not going to be honest with me, then you're no more trustworthy than anybody in there. Have a great night, Landon. Or don't, actually. I really don't give a shit."

I walked toward the lobby without looking back, even though I'd let my stubbornness write a check the rest of me didn't want to cash. The extent of my plan had been to bluff about wanting to go explore on my own. In my determination to piss him off, I'd just agreed to walk blindly into a BDSM club full of apparent sexual predators at the worst, and masters of emotional manipulation at the best. *Nice one, Andi.*

I could sense Landon easily keeping pace with me. I knew if I stopped or hesitated, he'd take me by the arm again and try to talk me into staying with him.

So, I didn't stop.

I let stubbornness pull me forward like a leash tied to my neck.

I passed through the lobby, briefly catching a glimpse of his brother, James, sitting in his usual spot at the bar. I turned a corner, ducked through a black curtain, and found myself in a dark room filled with scentless smoke. I half-blindly felt my way around the wall until I found a door, which I pushed my way through.

In what felt like seconds, I'd stumbled my way from the lobby to a mysterious, dark ass room in a creepy BDSM club.

Wonderful.

I turned and felt for the door handle, then twisted the lock. A paranoid part of my mind wondered if I was locking myself *in* with someone or something, but I pushed that thought away.

"What do we have here?" asked a man's voice from the darkness behind me.

I twitched back at the sudden sound. "Sorry," I said. "I'm just trying to avoid this guy who was bothering me. I'll be out of your hair in a minute or two."

Landon knocked on the door a few times and tried the handle.

"Andi," he called through the door. "Don't be stupid. Open the door. You don't know what you just walked into."

I squinted into the dark room and tried to find the person who had spoken. "Do you have a name, guy in the shadows?"

From what I could see, the room wasn't very large, but the only light was coming from a single bulb that didn't appear to work like normal light bulbs. I could see that it was on, but all it managed to illuminate were a few vague, fuzzy impressions I thought must be the walls of the room. If anything, I thought I'd have been able to see more if the light was off.

"I'm Edward."

I flinched back when I saw the man emerge from the shadows. He was almost as tall as Landon. He was broad, powerful, and he made all my instincts to run fire off at once.

"I should go, sorry," I said, reaching for the door.

"No," he said. Before I could unlock the door, his hand was on mine. Something about the way I hadn't even heard him *run*—which I was sure he did to cover the distance so fast—made my blood feel like ice. "You really shouldn't," he said. "We'd love to have you join us."

I looked behind him but couldn't see who the "we" he was talking about was. My skin crawled, like dozens of pairs of unseen eyes could be prying into me from the darkened corners of the room—phantom hands and fingers exploring my body in an unwelcome barrage.

"I'm going," I said more firmly. "So please back the fuck off and let me unlock the door."

"Andi? Who's in there?" Landon called from the other side of the door. "Open the door!"

"Creeper alert!" I called as loudly as I could.

Landon immediately started banging something hard into the door so that it flexed against its hinges. Edward made no sign of wanting to remove his hand from the lock, so I did the most reasonable thing I could think of. I put my hands on his shoulders, pulled down, and used the leverage to drive my knee up toward his crotch as hard as I could.

Instead of the soft collision with his balls I was looking for, my thigh was stopped by the palm of his hands.

"Word of advice," he said. "Putting your hands on the shoulders gives away your plan. Next time, just use the knee."

"Landon!" I called, a little more desperately. "Creeper alert. Defcon one, or whichever is the worst defcon level!"

There was a loud bang and the door finally cracked off its hinges. Landon shouldered his way in and put his arm between Edward and me.

For a few painfully tense moments, neither man said a word.

"This one yours?" Edward asked finally.

"Yes," Landon said.

The cold certainty in his voice gave me chills. Any other time, I probably would've butted in with some smartass comment to the contrary. But right now, I only felt a glow of comfort in knowing Landon was here to keep Edward and his creepy hands away from me.

Edward studied us for a few moments, as if trying to detect whether Landon was telling the truth. "Name your price."

"She's not for sale. Or for trade. She's mine." His tone brokered no argument.

Another wave of chills. *Sale or trade?* What the actual fuck? I was starting to think Landon may have been right when he said I didn't know what I was getting into by coming here alone. I was also starting to wonder if I really knew Grandpa Willy at all.

"Everything has a price. We'll just have to see what yours is. *I want this one,*" he tried to reach to touch my arm, but Landon swatted his hand away.

Edward chuckled. "Always so tense." He turned his attention to me, and his eyes grew predatory. "Sydney did mention you were playing with a new toy. *Hello, toy.*"

I cringed back.

Landon put his hand on my chest and urged me back toward the door. "Sydney has no idea what she's talking about. And if I even think you're planning on touching Andi again, I'll break both your hands. *Then* I'll make sure you lose your coin. *All of you,*" he added, turning his gaze toward the darkness.

I felt another cold shiver. This Edward guy was creepy enough. How many more like him were lurking just beyond the light? And what the hell were they doing before I came into the room, sitting in the dark and telling scary stories?

"That's a dangerous path," Edward said. "You're sure that's the stance you want to take?"

"Positive."

"Can we go?" I whispered.

Landon glared at Edward for a few more seconds, then nodded. "Come on," he said gruffly.

For once, I followed him without complaint and let him lead me back through the smoky room, the black curtain, down a winding hallway, and through a padded leather door. We were in what looked like an ordinary—if almost laughably gothic —bedroom.

I shook my head once we were inside and alone. "You take me straight to a bedroom, huh? If you think I'm going to just jump your bones because you saved me back there, you're—"

"No," he said. "I just wanted a quiet place where we can talk."

I crossed my arms. "Okay. Let's start with what the hell that was? And how many people were in that fucking room? You were talking to the shadows like you knew there were people there."

"That was Edward Kraft. He's... a necessary evil."

I bulged my eyes and spread my hands. "And that means, what? You know he's a creep, but you let him come to the club anyway? Or like how superheroes would go out of business if there were no supervillains? Because that's bullshit. Superheroes could help people on moving day, with taxes, and way more practical stuff. Supervillains—"

"It means part of the purpose of the club is to let everybody have a safe place to experience whatever BDSM is to them. For Edward, it's his harem."

"His harem..." I said slowly. "Correct me if I'm wrong, but isn't that like when a king has a swarm of fuck buddies at his disposal?"

"Something like that. Edward recruits women, and sometimes men he takes a liking to. They're all submissive to him. He wanted you to join. That's all."

"That's all. He just wanted to bully me into joining his sex slave club?"

"Despite what it seemed like; he knows the rules of the club. Nothing would've happened if you didn't sign a contract."

"Why don't you sound entirely convinced you're telling me the truth?"

Landon sighed. "Because I'm not sure anymore. There have been some rumors about Edward's tactics swirling around the club these past few weeks. Rumors that he's starting to act like he's above the rules, or that he thinks he knows—just never mind. The point is I've got it handled."

"Then take away his *coin*, or whatever that was you were talking about. You're in charge, aren't you?"

"Being in charge of a place like this isn't a ticket to ultimate power. There are sects. Groups of influence. Above all of that, there's the idea that nobody should feel singled out for their kink. People who lean toward Edward's tastes see him as a kind of leader. So, if I got rid of him, I'd be setting the kind of precedent that could destroy the club and what it stands for. The price of feeling accepted for our oddities is having to accept everyone else for theirs."

I pursed my lips and nodded thoughtfully. "I see. You just walk around and talk like you're tough, but when it comes down to doing something, you're afraid of making waves."

Landon's features darkened. "No. I'm reluctant to sabotage a club I've devoted most of my life to build. Edward is a situation I'm aware of, and it's one I'm monitoring. *Closely.*"

I walked to the edge of the bed and sat. "So, am I supposed to believe my grandfather really wanted me to learn the ins and outs of this place so I could take it over? Even though running it apparently sounds more like being a prison warden than a business manager?"

Landon shrugged. "I can't say why he wanted you to be involved. Maybe he wanted you to have a chance to see what I do. He might have thought you'd decide to leave me in my position once you saw what running the club entailed."

"Or maybe that's the angle you're pushing."

Landon sat down on the edge of the bed. For the first time since I'd known him, he looked exhausted as he stared down at his hands. When he finally looked up at me, none of the usual iron was in his expression. He looked more human. *More vulnerable.*

"Andi," he said. "About what you said in the hall. I've been as honest with you as I can be."

I squinted. "That's a lot of words that don't really say much."

Landon's jaw flexed. "What I mean is I'm trying my best."

"Take your time, if you're keeping something from me, it's like a wall. Maybe knocking it down will squish us, but keeping it up is sure as hell going to keep us apart."

Landon chuckled. "You're better at metaphors than me."

"I'm better at jokes than you, too. Some might argue that means my intelligence is superior."

"I wouldn't disagree."

We sat there in silence long enough for me to wonder if I was supposed to get up and leave. Maybe it would've been the smart thing to do. My brain knew to keep Landon at arm's length, but every moment I spent with him was a war with my body, which had entirely different plans.

Instead of leaving, which is what I should've done, I spoke. "Trust is hard for me, I guess. I think I stopped trusting myself to care about anyone or anything new. I lost my mom, then my dad, and now my grandpa." I tried to smile to soften the melodrama of saying it all out loud, but my lips quivered. I cleared my throat and put my hand to my lips, hopefully in a way that didn't make it obvious I was trying to hide. "It doesn't get easier," I said a little shakily. "Losing people, you care about, I mean. So it feels like the only rational thing is to stop caring in the first place. The more you let yourself care, the more you wind up getting hurt in the end."

Landon nodded. "I guess different paths can lead people to that same conclusion."

I looked up. "Did you lose someone, too?" I asked. I didn't think that was what he meant, but he seemed so reluctant to talk about what was on his mind. I knew I needed to prod him a little to get it out.

"Yes." He looked at me for a long time, face scrunched like he was trying to bring himself to say something. Finally, he hung his head and shook it. "I lost him twice. Once when he gave up on us and once when he died. But the first time was the real death. The second time just meant whatever little hope of things getting better was gone for good."

I waited for him to say more, but felt my stomach sink even with the little he was telling me. I hadn't realized his father was dead, too. From the little he'd told me at the aquarium, I'd been able to piece together a slightly less incomplete puzzle. Still, my understanding of Landon and his past was full of holes.

"I'm so sorry," I said. I reached out and took his hand in mine. It was rough, warm, and surprisingly hard.

"No, don't be. I wasn't trying to one-up you. I just wanted you to understand that I know where you're coming from, even if it's not for the same reasons. Trusting people is hard. It makes you vulnerable. And I know this probably doesn't mean much, but you can trust me. Finish the list, and I'll make sure you get your share of the hotel."

I studied Landon, trying to see through to the boy he must've been growing up. I imagined how he had probably stalked the halls of his high school with a personality as sharp and deadly as a knife. I thought of the throngs of girls who must've been desperate to throw themselves on that edge, even if they knew the best they could hope for was a scar they'd be able to tell their friends about.

Tragedy or not, I imagined he had been the boy who was always stronger, better, and faster than everyone else. He was probably the one teachers let get away with every little thing because even they weren't immune to the awe he practically oozed.

And now all that tragedy and privilege had shaped him into this frightening combination of charm and coldness. The closest comparison I could think of was that it felt like looking at a gorgeous painting while ominous music played in the background. As much as you could trust your eyes that what you saw was pretty and pure, you still couldn't help but let that chilling music twist your perception.

"Tell me this," I said. "Are you a bad person?"

He looked at me, almost sadly. "Yes."

"And what do you really want from me?"

"Everything."

I licked my lips. "What if I told you I have gonorrhea; would you want that too?"

Landon didn't even flinch. "There it is."

"There what is?"

"I've finally made you nervous enough to get a joke out of you. Here's what I think. I think you're nervous because you know you're going to submit to me before long. And you're scared that you'll like it. But you want to hate it, just to spite me."

"Those are a lot of assumptions. What if I just want to feel like I can trust you before I give you a piece of my heart to play with?"

Landon's eyes were like glinting coals in the dark room. He moved closer, one hand cupping my cheek and the other on my thigh.

I shivered against the sudden contact. I almost recoiled back, but I couldn't make myself do it. His touch was the most delicious kind of sin.

His mouth was just inches from mine again, but his eyes bore into me. "I want to make you moan my name. I want you to say it until you're hoarse and your muscles are shaking with need. I want to feel you shudder against me as you come."

Each word that came from his cruel and perfect lips was like an impact in my chest, forcing more and more air out of my lungs with each syllable. By the end, I was breathless. "So, you're saying you think I'm cute," I whispered.

There it was again. I was waving a pathetic attempt at humor over my head like a little white flag. Meanwhile, all around me, bombshells were exploding—stinging my cheeks with dirt and shrapnel. Despite it all, I had to sling out a stupid joke, or at least a bit of sarcasm.

The difference between Landon and everybody else was that he plowed straight over my humor. It slid past him like a harmless breeze. He just kept coming. *Kept advancing.* He made me think of that scene in *Terminator 2* when the T-1000 was chasing down John and Sarah Connor in their car. No matter how many shots they fired at him or how many twists and turns they took, he just kept coming. And when hands weren't good enough to hold on, he morphed his entire arms into metal things with hooks on the end. And yes, they eventually shot those off and lost him, but everybody watching the movie knew that wasn't the end. Even if they couldn't see him in the rearview, he'd be coming. Always in pursuit. Always advancing.

"I would be bad for you," he said, almost gently. "I'd want to punish you for being such a pain in my ass, but the worst part would only come once I'd shown you how badly you want me."

"That pain in your ass could be hemorrhoids," I said. "Staring at your phone on the toilet? Straining? It can happen to anyone. They say you shouldn't spend more than five minutes at a time on there."

Landon didn't so much as blink, then he straightened, letting me feel like I could breathe again when he wasn't acting like he was about to pounce on me. "I know you're hearing all of this. And it doesn't matter what words come out of that pretty little mouth of yours. Your pupils are dilated like your entire body is flooding with adrenaline, and..." he tapped my knee and I flinched like I'd just been shocked. "You're wound as tight as a wire. So do I need to keep reading you, or are you ready to talk to me. To *actually* talk to me."

I cleared my throat. "Maybe my adrenaline is pumping because I'm pissed off."

"Could be," he reached out and softly pulled my hand away from my lips, which I had been absentmindedly rubbing with my thumb. "But people tend to touch their lips when they're aroused."

"You're a body language expert, too? Tell me. What does it mean if somebody's foot is touching your balls at a high speed? Do you want me to demonstrate?"

He showed no reaction to my threat. The frustrating part was that it really did seem as if he could see straight through all my bluffs. "Every time we're together, you can't help talking about my balls. I think people in the world of psychology would call that a fixation."

I gritted my teeth. "There's a difference between touching something and kicking it."

"Yes, exactly. Because touching can be torture just as much as pain can be ecstasy."

"Uh, no. That wasn't really the point I was trying to make."

"Here's what I think. The only way I can get honesty out of you is from these." He sat down beside me on the bed and turned my head to face him, rubbing his thumb across my lips.

I didn't see him moving, but Landon's face was closer to mine. No matter what words were coming out of my mouth, he was right. I couldn't stop looking at his lips—hungry for another taste of the explosion I'd felt in the hallway.

Landon's eyes told me everything. He was going to kiss me again. *Worse*, I wanted him to, secrets or not. I even felt my chin tilting up and my eyes starting to close. The last thing I saw was the satisfied, knowing smirk on his mouth.

Then our lips met more softly this time. It wasn't the violent attack in the hallway. It was more careful, probing. It almost felt like he really could somehow read my thoughts with the kiss, and this was a physical conversation. Each flick and roll of our tongues was a message that he read loud and clear.

His big hands cradled my cheeks and I knew how easy it would be to lay backwards and let him practically fall on top of me.

The scariest part was how my worries and doubts melted with his lips and hands on me. They felt like wisps of smoke that I could see, but not grasp. I didn't *want* to feel them. All I wanted was this.

Him.

Now.

I wanted it to last forever so I wouldn't have to go back to that world where Landon was real and so were the doubts I had about him. The fear that he was going to make me care for him just in time to smash my heart to pieces.

I put my hands on his chest to push him away, but the warm hardness of his muscles made me pause.

God.

I'd never felt so out of control in my own body. My brain was like a little, insignificant pilot trying to run a complex machine —only I'd suddenly forgotten what all the buttons do and every moment spun the situation farther and farther out of my control.

"Landon," I breathed.

"What?" His dark hair had fallen partly over his eyes and it physically hurt to see how good he looked—to know I was going to do the only thing I could think of to avoid getting carried away by the dangerous momentum I felt.

"Thank you." I pushed his chest gently, but firmly enough that he got the message and leaned back. "Now I know what a mistake tastes like. I'd always wondered."

His eyes smoldered, but I didn't let myself sink into his trap. I stood, hoped I hadn't left an embarrassing wet spot of arousal from where I'd sat on the bed, and hurried to the door.

"When do you want to sign the contract?" he asked calmly.

Right now. I want to do whatever it takes to get your hands back on me and the taste of your lips on my tongue again. I want it all, even if I'm almost certain I'll regret every moment of it. "How about never?" I said, slamming the door behind me.

I WAS CURLED IN MY FAVORITE CHAIR—THE ONE IN THE LOBBY where I'd read hundreds of books growing up. Today, the story was of a golden-skinned alien smuggler with a massive, heat-seeking cock. The cargo he was smuggling happened to be a virgin Earthling woman, and his twelve-inch coke can cock was absolutely going to find its way to her. I grinned to myself when I imagined what Landon would think of a book like this.

Except I didn't have to imagine for long. He was walking straight toward me. For once, he wasn't wearing a suit. He'd dressed down in a nice button-up shirt with the collar loose and the sleeves rolled up. His forearms were muscular and covered in tattoos, which, from our time at the dolphin encounter, I knew snaked across half of his chest as well.

"I expected you to hide from me for a week or so," he said, sitting himself down in the chair beside mine. "It's almost disappointing to find you so easily. And not even twenty-four hours since I last saw you."

"Maybe I just hoped you wouldn't be pathetic enough to come looking for me this quickly."

"The contract is waiting for your signature. We can't move forward unless you sign it."

I tried to look annoyed. The truth was I'd spent all night tormenting myself with vivid, dirty dreams about what would've happened if I'd signed that contract. I imagined Landon carrying me to demented sex tables in dark rooms—tying me up and using more than just his breath to torment me.

The most embarrassing element of the whole thing was that my conflicting feelings somehow made the idea of his touch all the more appealing. He was the forbidden fruit hanging from the tree—at least if forbidden fruits had six packs, tattoos, and jawlines like razor blades. And no, I hadn't fully committed to pulling the fruit off the tree, per se. But I had basically licked it, sniffed it, stuck my tongue down its throat, and maybe even taken a nibble.

"What happens if I change my mind after signing it?"

"Good. So you're considering it. And if you change your mind, you'll have the only copy of the contract. Just tear it up and we're done. It's much less about legality and more about the formality of defining your boundaries."

I mimicked a large box around myself and gave him a dry look. "That's my boundary. You on the outside of it, me on the inside."

"No," he said. "This would be more nuanced."

"It was a joke," I said.

"If I stopped to indulge all of your 'jokes,' we would never be able to finish a conversation."

I sighed. "That's a decent point."

"Do you want to meet me in the club to sign it, or would you be more comfortable in your room?"

"I don't remember agreeing to anything."

"Do you want to give up your inheritance?"

I glared. "Sometimes, I can't decide if I should be pissed at you for statements like that or at my grandpa."

"Hate whoever you like but make a decision."

I wondered how he'd feel if my decision was to throw a lemon in his eye. One thing was for sure, he'd have trouble looking so frustratingly calm and collected with a bit of citric acid in his sinuses. "How about this? I take *you* on a date this time. If I'm not scared off by the end of it, I'll sign your contract."

"A second date, then? Correct me if I'm wrong, but isn't that the one where you usually come?"

Blood rushed to my cheeks. "It usually doesn't snow in Florida, but that doesn't mean it has never happened."

"What?"

"Forget it. And no, this would be a first date, because I still never agreed to call the aquarium a date."

Landon looked like he was trying to decide if he'd accept my little diversion. I could tell he was practically chomping at the bit to get me to sign his contract. "What sort of date?"

"Does it matter?"

14

LANDON

Andi was playing with fire. First, she'd strung me along and assumed I'd give her as much time as she wanted to finish William's list. Then, she'd been in no particular hurry to sign my contract. And now? Now she had the nerve to tell me we'd go on this little date of hers in *two days*.

I wanted to growl with annoyance. In part, I just didn't like when I wasn't the one in control. The other part of me... Well, that part just wanted to have her to myself again, and sooner, rather than later.

Of course, there were also two very large problems between me and what I wanted. One was the inconvenient truth about my father, AKA Andi's "grandfather." The other was that the more I came to appreciate her, the more trouble I had forgiving myself for thinking I deserved her. I was just the bastard using every excuse I had to manipulate her into spending more time with me. Even if I got what I wanted and she started to have feelings for me, I'd be building one lie on top of another.

I stopped by the apartment to check on mom and found Grant sitting on the love seat. He was in the middle of a story. If it was anything like his usual stories, it was probably at least ninety percent fabricated.

Grant was something between a business partner and a friend who ran the Platinum Pecker, the third sister club to the Golden Pecker.

When he saw me, he stood and clasped my hand tight. He was dark haired and built like he'd spent his life trekking through the Outback on foot, wrestling wild animals. Although I knew he'd only actually lived in Australia until he was about five. He didn't even have an accent, but something about him always did seem to scream "Australia" to me.

"Do I want to know why you're here?" I asked.

"Grant was just telling me about when he used to lead safaris," mom said, punctuating her sentence with a hacking cough.

"Bullshitting, you mean," I said.

Grant gave me a careless shrug. "I'm a storyteller. You don't hear Jeff R Martin apologizing for entertaining people with his books, do you?"

"George," I said.

Grant gave me a puzzled look.

I decided trying to explain myself would only confuse him more. "You don't usually make house calls. What's going on?"

Grant gestured for me to follow him to the kitchen, which was about as far out of earshot as we could manage in the small apartment.

"Just wanted to let you know I've been hearing some rumors," Grant said once we were alone.

"About?"

"You. Your club. Some submissive you've been around with and that she's William's granddaughter. People are playing connect the dots. William dies. His granddaughter suddenly shows up in the club. Looks like you're showing her the ropes. Get what I'm getting at? My grams always said if it smells like shit and looks like shit, you probably don't need to bother tasting it to find out. *So...*"

I raised my eyebrows. "Your grams sounds like a charmer. But, no. I'm keeping the club. Andi's involvement is... complicated. It's not something I need to explain to the members, either."

"Wait," Grant said. "How exactly are you keeping the club? You and William hated each other. He'd never—"

"He did," I said. "Sort of."

Grant looked like he wanted to know more, but I didn't intend to give it.

He raised his eyebrows, then shook his head. "Just be careful. You lose the trust of your members, and you'll be in charge of a big ass, empty building."

"Yeah, well there's nothing I can do about it unless I want to ruin things with Andi." I knew that statement wouldn't make a ton of sense given the information Grant had, but it was the truth.

Grant suddenly smiled like an idiot and punched my shoulder. "Look at you. *Smitten.* I've seen it before—in other men, of course. The only thing I've ever seen you smitten with is an expensive suit." He tugged on my lapel as if to emphasize the point.

I slapped his hand away. "Okay. Yes. I care about Andi, and probably more than I should given how little time I've actually spent with her. But it's complicated between us, and complicated things have a way of breaking before long."

Grant held up his forefinger in dramatic fashion, looking at it with two wide eyes. Then he followed it as he made a circle with his other hand and inserted the forefinger inside. "Not complicated, Landon. I can show you again, if you're still confused on the details."

I sighed. "There's a reason I don't visit the Platinum Pecker more often."

"Yeah, because I make you pay a cover fee and you're too broke to afford it."

I grinned. "Please don't rub in the fact that you didn't have to pay the blood relative tax. It only makes me hate you more than I already do."

"So," Grant said. "What's so complicated about it?"

"She doesn't know William was my father, for starters."

Grant pulled his lips back, wincing. "Goddamn, you're not a smart man. Are you?"

"I never found the right time to tell her."

"The right time would have been probably in the first or second sentence you ever uttered to her. Maybe, 'hey, I'm Landon and my dad was actually your adoptive grandfather.'"

"I didn't expect to be in her life for more than a few minutes. By the time I realized, it had already gone too far."

"And so, it's complicated now because you're still letting it go further? Just tell her, man. The longer you wait, the worse it's going to be. Hell, you're probably already screwed, anyway."

"Thanks for the comforting words," I said dryly. "I'm going to tell her. I'm just waiting for the right time."

Grant pursed his lips and nodded. "I can see that. If I knew I was going to die, I would probably take a few minutes to choose where it was going to happen."

"Don't you have some sort of work to be doing?"

He shrugged. "I'll be happy to head out. If I hang around you much longer, I'm bound to get splattered when the shitstorm arrives. And make no mistake, you're about to be in the mother of all shitstorms."

I watched him go but couldn't help thinking he was right. I needed to tell Andi the truth *and* I needed to handle the rumors swirling around us.

I hated that my selfish brain went straight to what she might do if she decided to cut ties after I told her the truth. Would she know she could hurt me by talking to the right people in the club? If she talked to my ex, Sydney, or Edward, she could probably give them enough ammunition to chase away every last member of The Golden Pecker. The most logical thing to do would be to go finalize things with the lawyers now. I could cement my role as the owner of The Golden Pecker, transfer my share of William's hotel to her, and *then* deal with the messy truth.

There was only one problem with that plan.

Despite what I might have said to Andi, I still wasn't completely convinced that I had it in me to ignore William's wishes. Sure, I hated him for what he'd done to us. But somehow, I had begun to feel like lying and sidestepping the terms of the agreement would put a gulf between Andi and I that I'd never be able to cross.

If I tried to protect what flimsy hope there was of something meaningful forming between Andi and I, I'd be putting my mom's future and her treatment at risk.

I raked my hands through my hair and tried my hardest to think of another way.

15

ANDI

Landon met me at the zoo around noon. He had left behind the suit in favor of a black coat and jeans. As good as he looked dressed up, I enjoyed seeing him in something a little more casual, too. After all, Landon didn't need any help looking professional or intimidating. I thought he probably could've strolled into a board meeting in a t-shirt and jeans and still commanded the room.

"Wow," I said, noting the look on his face when he arrived. "Did you just finish punching some newborn kittens, or something?"

Landon's frown deepened. "Why would I punch newborn kittens?"

"You just look... *dark*. Like somebody told you they canceled Wheel of Fortune for good."

"Believe it or not, I'd survive that news unscathed."

I pursed my lips and shrugged. "Then you're a monster with poor taste. But seriously, what's up?"

Landon studied a patch of wet cement between us. If I didn't know better, I'd say he was nervous. Nervousness and Landon together made about as much sense as gifting a snake a pair of boots and mittens for Christmas, so my curiosity spiked.

"Know what?" I said, cutting him off just as he was about to speak. "I don't want to start our first official date with the gloomies. Forget I asked. And hey, I saw how you were practically a kid in a candy shop at the aquarium. The zoo is probably right up your alley, isn't it?"

The darkness in his expression still didn't fade completely, but he made the effort of forcing a smile for me. "Guilty as charged."

"I should also mention that I am extremely well connected around here. I pulled a few strings and arranged for us to have a private elephant encounter." I mimicked blowing some dust off my fingernails and then brushed my shoulder.

Landon's smile looked a little more genuine now. "You're making that up, right?"

I flashed a smug smile. "I guess you'll just have to wait and see, won't you?"

Little by little, Landon's mood improved throughout the morning. We started with the monkeys. When one of the gorillas pooped in his own hand, then smeared it on his head, I thought Landon was going to gag. A few minutes later, a bonobo threw up in its own hand and started eating it, at which point Landon really did gag.

I laughed as we retreated from the primate section of the zoo. Landon looked pale, but he was at least grinning faintly.

"I wouldn't have pegged you for someone with a weak stomach."

"I've never liked monkeys. They're like twisted, evil little naked humans."

I burst out with a surprised laugh. "Definitely not. Most of them are super sweet. It's more like they are freakishly strong toddlers."

"Right. Because a toddler who can rip your arms off and beat you to death with them isn't one of the most horrible things I can imagine."

By the time we had fed the giraffes and watched the penguins fail to shuffle out of their exhibit because the ones at the front kept falling and knocking the others down like bowling pins, Landon's mood was drastically improved.

I felt a little twinge of pride that I could cheer him up. I also felt strangely sad that he didn't seem to try to pick up where we left off. I only had myself to blame, of course. I'd told him kissing him was a mistake. I probably would've needed to worry if he was still trying to put moves on me. But a very stupid side of me still wanted him to try. It was like I couldn't forgive myself if I didn't at least try to push him away, but it didn't mean I wanted to succeed. I was playing a very dumb game of conditions with myself, where it wasn't the outcome that determined if I was a bad person—it was how I got there.

Neither of us were particularly hungry after the atrocities we saw from the monkeys, so we settled for ice creams, which we ate in a pretty area by the pond surrounded by flowers.

"How am I doing?" Landon asked.

"Well," I reached up and wiped a little smear of chocolate ice cream from the tip of his nose, "you eat ice cream about as carefully as a small child." I licked the ice cream off my finger without thinking, then paused and blushed.

Landon's eyes were still on where I'd sucked the ice cream off my finger. "I was talking about your general level of comfort. This date was to convince yourself it wasn't crazy to finish the list with me, right?"

"I usually try not to sign sex contracts with men until the third date. So, if I end up signing that thing after only two, you'll know you did really well."

Landon chuckled. "I thought you weren't counting the aquarium as a date. But hey, I'll take it."

"So, why here? Other than your inside connection."

"I was serious. You looked so happy at the aquarium. I just figured you were an animal lover and..."

Landon was smiling.

"What?"

"It's just interesting," he said. "Women I've dated... They don't —" he paused, running his tongue over his teeth and frowning at something. "I appreciate this. It was thoughtful. I'm more used to lazy flourishes—like front row tickets to a basketball game or something."

"You're welcome. But don't give me too much credit. I'm too broke for a lazy flourish. Being piss poor does wonders for your creativity," I said. "So, I was right? You're super into animals, aren't you? Do you know all the scientific names and that kind of thing? Habitats, mating patterns?"

"Not exactly," he said. "The truth is my thing with the aquarium is a little more sentimental than anything else."

He focused on his ice cream, as if he was going to get away with dropping that little nugget of curiosity and moving on.

"Sentimental how?" I asked.

Landon looked up, and it was clear he was deciding whether he wanted to go into more detail. Finally, he licked his lips, wadded up his napkin, and set it inside his ice cream bowl. "My brother and I had a little bit of an up and down childhood. Mostly it was because our dad could never decide if he wanted to be a shitty father or a good one. But I had this birthday one year. I was turning nine, and I guess he'd been shitty for a couple months and the guilt got to him. So he took me to that aquarium, just me and him. Normally, he'd just kind of complain at places like that or find somewhere to get a beer and zone out while he let us wander."

"That time though," Landon said. His eyes had gone distant, like he was seeing it in his mind. "He stayed with me the whole time. Didn't touch a drop of alcohol. He read the plaques to me, told me about the animals, and even paid the extra money for the dolphin encounter. It wasn't like him at all, and I just remember all day I couldn't stop thinking about how I wanted to kind of bottle it up. I knew the shitty ones were going to come again, but I thought if I could just sort of capture that moment, I could live with it."

When he stopped talking and looked at me, he seemed to realize what he'd just said. Landon laughed at himself. "Sorry. That all sounds really pathetic. Doesn't it?"

"No," I said. "It doesn't." I suddenly felt like the world's biggest asshole for teasing him about liking the aquarium. I was also fairly sure he was just being nice about liking the zoo visit, too. "Jesus," I said suddenly. "And I bring you here, which probably just makes you think about all that. I'm sorry. We can go somewhere else if you want."

"I'm happy right here."

Our eyes met, and as a few seconds ticked by, it felt like his words began to take on new meaning. I found myself smiling and biting my lip. "Well," I said. "Do you want to get up close and personal with some elephants?"

"You really were serious about that?"

"When it comes to elephants, I don't joke around."

As promised, one of Bree's best friends, Luna, let us sneak into the elephant enclosure a little while later. We got to hand feed the baby elephant, hose them down, and even sit on the leg of an adult elephant to pose for pictures. Landon tried to scowl when I made him pose with me, but I could tell he was enjoying himself.

We thanked Luna when it was over and walked back toward the exit. It felt like neither of us knew exactly what to do. I didn't want the night to be over yet, but I also didn't want to weird him out by suggesting we go walk around and look at the same exhibits again. So we headed for the exit in relative silence.

When we reached the parking lot, I was still thinking about his comment. *I'm happy right here.* What surprised me most about it was how good it felt to know I had made him happy. The more I learned about Landon, the more I saw how broken he must be on the inside. I liked that I could be the one to help him forget about all the pain in his past. There was still something he wasn't telling me, but I was making progress, which was starting to feel like it was enough, for now.

"Well," Landon said when we reached the point where we'd both need to head separate ways. My Uber was waiting, and his car was parked farther back. The poor side of me had considered taking him up on his offer to give me a ride, but the practical part of me had been worried the pressure to go back to his place with him when our day was over would be too great.

"Well," I said, bobbing up and down on my tiptoes a few times.

"Final verdict?" he asked.

I made a show of thinking hard. "I'll *look* at the contract. No promises about signing it."

Landon nodded, but once again, he seemed distracted.

"Is something wrong?"

He furrowed his brows. Just before he spoke, my Uber driver leaned out of the window.

"You almost ready?" the driver asked. "I'm going to miss out on peak hours in the city if we don't get rolling."

Landon waved me off. "Go ahead. Meet me at the club tomorrow night?"

"Yeah," I said, smiling. "Sounds good."

There was a moment of awkwardness. It almost felt like I should lean in and give him a kiss, but he turned to leave before I could make a decision.

I spent the ride back to the hotel thinking about everything, but by the time I arrived, I didn't feel closer to understanding anything.

. . .

LANDON SAT BEHIND A LARGE, HIGHLY POLISHED DESK IN HIS OFFICE within The Golden Pecker. I squinted at him from across the desk, wondering how long he planned to sit and scribble something on a notepad.

If nothing else, it gave me time to think. Particularly, I was most interested in trying to puzzle out where he and I stood now. Usually, two dates, two mindblowing kisses, and an impromptu bondage session would've made me think we were a couple.

But we weren't a couple. I knew it wasn't that simple, partly because I'd made a solid effort to dispel that idea after our second kiss. Current me wasn't sure I was exactly pleased with past me for that one, but maybe it was for the best. I enjoyed being around him, sometimes because he was so easy to irritate when he was trying to be all serious. But other times, I couldn't help falling into the age-old trap of wanting to fix him.

For all his apparent success, Landon seemed broken. His rougher side was more like scar tissue—a protective layer of shielding that hadn't had the chance to heal fully. Then again, I guess scars never really healed, which would mean my analogy only illustrated how much I was wasting my time.

"Where do you even find a sweater like that?" he finally asked.

Just because I'd wanted to rile him up, I'd worn my lazy reading outfit of sweatpants and an oversized unicorn sweater. Yes, it even had a plushy, glittery gold horn that jutted out of my chest. He'd had to walk me through the whole club while I was wearing it, and I hoped it had embarrassed him.

I actually had an entire stockpile of sweaters like this, but I had been a little too embarrassed to bring Landon in on my collection. Until now.

"The internet," I said. "But I had to sew the horn on myself." I gave it a little flick, which made it wobble suggestively.

Landon rolled his eyes, grinning.

"So, did you have me come here to admire your penmanship, or are you going to show me the contract?"

He loosened his tie and pulled it free, then unbuttoned his collar. I felt my traitorous eyes scanning his neckline for hints of the tanned, muscled flesh I knew lay beneath.

"Please, make yourself comfortable," I said. "If your pants are bothering you, why not toss those off too? And who needs underwear, right?"

"I can put my tie back on if you're too distracted to focus."

I sighed. "No. Go on."

He nodded, running a hand through his hair before opening the first page of the contract for me.

"Some of the verbiage here—out of context," he added carefully. "It may not be terminology you're used to. The important thing to remember is this is more of a formality so we can establish your hard boundaries now, without intruding on the moment down the line."

I watched him with a skeptically raised eyebrow. "This sounds ridiculous. You know that, right?"

"So long as this contract is in effect," he continued, once again ignoring me. "You will be my... *property*."

Now my eyebrows were threatening to slide up into my hairline. "Is this some of that 'verbiage' you warned me about?"

"Yes."

"Why would somebody willingly agree to be the property of somebody else?"

"It's intentionally worded in a way that is difficult to swallow. Ultimately, the idea is you'd agree to become my submissive. *In this club*, you would be like my property. Outside The Golden Pecker, none of this contract would apply, unless we wished."

"And how do you treat your property?" I asked, even though I could hardly believe I was still considering this. The truth was, I didn't just want to keep exploring the list because of the potential inheritance. Actually, the real truth was there was no amount of money that would've made me go through a list like this. Landon was the little flickering flame of interest that kept me coming back, and over time, it was becoming less of a spark and more of a wildfire. I'd felt something when I was under his control at the aquarium and when I was sitting beside him in The Red Room. I'd felt a dirty, exhilarating thrill that I still craved more of.

"In this case," Landon said. "I would treat her delicately, even if she had a sour mouth and an inability to take anything seriously."

"My mouth tasted sour?" I asked, blushing.

Landon's eyes flicked up at that. I thought I even saw the hint of a smirk. "I was talking about the words that come out of it. But no. You tasted..." He trailed off, then sat up a little straighter. We hadn't talked about our kiss from the other night in the club, and the subject seemed to make him as uncomfortable as it made me.

"I just take dental hygiene very seriously," I said. "So, if I had bad breath, I'd have wanted to know. Floss, brush, mouthwash. People don't realize you're supposed to floss first, but, yeah. You knock all those particles out from between your teeth *after* brushing and they just sit in there, causing mayhem. Gingivitis is no joke," I added quietly.

Landon was watching me with a flicker of amusement behind his eyes. "You're nervous. Nervous that you're going to accept the terms of this contract, even though it frightens you. Nervous that you'll like it."

"I've only heard the first sentence of the thing."

Landon read through the rest of the contract, collecting and marking my preferences. In some cases, I had to answer that I didn't know if I'd enjoy something, like having my toes sucked on, because no guy had ever decided to try that. I even had to describe spots on my body that were particularly ticklish, as well as go over my medical history. There were a few boxes I noticed Landon made a check mark in the "No" box without even asking my preference.

"What are those?" I asked.

"Things I don't participate in, even if my submissive requested them."

"You mean there's something too pervy, even for you?"

"Everybody has their preferences."

I pursed my lips. *Fine.* Be mysterious. I stared at him as he clinically finished going through the contract, including several prying questions about my sexual history.

"Can I ask you something?"

"You can ask, but I may choose not to answer," he said.

"Why do you want this club so badly? Couldn't you just start your own without having to worry about the shadow of my grandfather hanging over it? Or some other kind of business?"

He didn't answer right away. I saw that familiar look on his face—the one I saw every time I knew he was struggling to dig the truth up from somewhere deep. "Because I don't have the money to start my own. And I need the money this club generates."

I tilted my head. "But your car... your clothes. You're loaded, right?"

He looked ashamed, shaking his head. "Your grandfather was careful to make sure I could appear that way, yes. But he was also petty enough to only pay me the bare minimum to keep food on my table. Everything else is technically his property, even now."

"Why?" I asked. I wasn't sure I believed him—like the person he was talking about couldn't be the Grandpa Willy I'd known my whole life.

"That's a story I'm not ready to share. *Not yet,*" he added.

I frowned. More and more, I suspected the story had something to do with me, even if I couldn't piece together how that would be possible. I decided I was nearly done being patient with him. Maybe I was wrong, and I had no business knowing his secrets, but I did know I was the one putting my neck on the line with him. It was my heart that was in danger of getting smashed to pieces, and I wasn't willing to be vulnerable forever.

"Fine," I said. "But you need to find a way to tell me. *Soon,*" I added.

When the time finally came for me to ink my name at the bottom of the list, I couldn't help looking up at the man sitting across from me. As usual, he seemed to attract the shadows so that his otherwise perfect features took on a sinister turn.

Landon tapped his finger impatiently on the line with the red "X" beside it. "Are you going to sign?"

I picked up the pen, gave him one last glare for good measure, and wrote down my name.

16

LANDON

Grant found me in my office at The Golden Pecker, where I was going over the latest financial figures. The club was wildly profitable, which was thanks to the way William had decided to structure the memberships. Becoming a member of The Golden Pecker wasn't a right, it was a privilege, and it was a privilege only obscene amounts of money could buy. The eye-watering price had quickly turned The Golden Pecker into a status symbol that New York's wealthy elite needed to have attached to their name. Over seventy percent of our membership dues came from people who had never set foot inside the club more than once in the past year.

But they had the coin with the Golden Pecker emblem on it, which meant they got what they were paying for. And that meant our finances for the quarter were as ridiculous as usual.

I looked up at Grant expectantly. "Two visits in a single week?" I had a suspicion I knew why he'd come. I'd all but ignored the warning he had passed to me at the apartment a few days ago. I was letting the rumors boil and fester, and it was all because my situation with Andi made me feel paralyzed. It was like the Minesweeper game I used to play when I was a kid, only every available move nearly guaranteed I'd land on an explosive mine. The only play was to sit still for as long as I could.

My talent in managing The Golden Pecker had always been in how I handled the members. I let the eccentrics have their little corners to play with impunity. I kept the general membership happy with the sort of amenities and special treatment they wanted. I solved disputes in ways that left both parties happy more often than not. But this time, the only solution my members would approve of was the removal of Andi from the equation. That, or I could finalize the will and remove any possibility that Andi would inherit it. My gut told me making a move on the will would push Andi away, but waiting much longer might push my members to the brink of their patience.

"Have you decided what you're going to do?" Grant asked. "I'm assuming you haven't done anything yet, considering the rumors are only getting louder."

"I'm making sure my choice is the right one before I act," I said stonily.

"Yeah, well, there comes a point when planning the quickest escape from a burning building becomes an exercise in futility. You know, the point where the entire building is on fire and every exit is blocked?"

"I'm not out of options yet."

He gave my shoulder a squeeze. "But the door handles are heating up and there's smoke filling the stairwell. Also, you would hate to lose those leftovers in the breakroom, so you're going to have to detour for them before you make your escape."

I narrowed my eyes. "*What?*"

"Sorry," he said. "I'm just really hungry. I skipped lunch to be here. Speaking of," he wiggled his eyebrows, saluted, and left.

It was only a few seconds before I heard the clattering of glasses at the bar. *Idiot.* Admittedly, I liked the idiot, but I definitely didn't need to tell him that.

I did need to think about how I was going to deal with the

club, but every time I tried to focus, I could only see Andi and that stubborn glint in her eyes. Just thinking about tying her up again and watching her squirm for me made my dick stiffen.

Now that she'd signed the contract, she was officially my submissive. I knew she didn't completely understand what that entailed, but I planned to give her a real taste of it tonight.

All that was left to do was wait until she arrived.

17

ANDI

I went through the motions like it was a normal day. I helped write a post about whether you should have your baby wear a helmet in the crib for Rachel, read through one of Bree's college application letters, and listened to Aubria while she practiced explaining her dissertation to me.

Except I only felt half there. The other half of my mind kept replaying the moment I'd signed Landon's contract—the contract that made me his *property*. My imagination had run wild with what tonight was going to be like when I met him at the club.

And then it was time. My stomach felt like it was full of Pop Rocks and my stupid hands wouldn't stop sweating. Just after midnight, I sent a text to Landon, letting him know I was coming. I still didn't have a key, so he had to meet me at the secret entrance to the wine cellar and let me in.

His text came back a few moments later.

Landon: Looking forward to breaking you in.

I made an annoyed face at my phone. *Breaking me in?* If that's what he thought—

I angrily tapped out a response.

Andi: Good luck with that.

I found myself grinning as I reread our brief exchange, then wiped the smile off my face. Landon wasn't a grinning matter.

The door opened, and I was greeted by the frowning demon himself. "Took your time," he said.

"Judging by the scowl on your face, it looks like I took *your* time."

Apparently, Landon didn't appreciate my blinding wit, because all he did was gesture for me to come through the door. He stuck his arm out to stop me from going any further.

"Before we go in," he said. "We need to establish some ground rules."

"You were that kid growing up who had way too much fun explaining how games worked, weren't you? Everyone would show up for a game of tag, then half an hour later you'd probably still be covering what constitutes a tag and what doesn't." I did my best nerd impression, speaking through my nose. "Only if five fingers make full contact! And when I say five, I mean five!"

Landon had an arsenal of annoyed stares, and I thought the one he aimed at me now was of the mild annoyance category. "Are you ready to listen?"

I crossed my arms. "I'm just saying... Contracts. Rules. *More rules.* How complicated can this really be?"

"Think of it this way: you're walking across a narrow bridge with no railings. The contract is a safety harness."

"And the endless rules are, *what?* The medicine that makes you uncontrollably drowsy, so you fall asleep before stepping foot on the bridge?"

Landon took a calming breath, then, as was his way, he decided to ignore my comment entirely. "Inside the club, you will be my submissive. You will follow me everywhere I go, and you will not walk in front of me. Stay as close as you can, keep your eyes down, and absolutely avoid making eye contact with other men. Do nothing without my permission. Understand?"

I worked my lips to the side. "What if I need a bathroom break? Do I raise my hand? Two fingers? One?"

"You tell me you need to use the restroom."

"And what happens if you tell me to do something I don't want to do?"

"You use the safe word. It will be—"

"The geese flew south for the summer."

"What?"

"That can be our safe word. It's supposed to be something we wouldn't ever say by accident, right?"

"It's supposed to be a safe *word.* Not a safe ridiculous phrase. And the safe word isn't up for a vote. Yellow means you're uncomfortable, but willing to proceed. Red means stop."

"Boring. But fine."

"Now come with me. Remember, eyes down and follow close behind me. It's important that everyone else in the club knows your mine."

I hated how a little fluttering blast of nerves rose up at his words. *Mine.* I could make all the stupid jokes I wanted, but inside, I was absolutely freaking out. Despite the contract and the extensive rules briefings, I still had no idea what I was getting into. I hardly even remembered all the things Grandpa Willy read off on his list.

"Red!" I half-shouted.

Landon turned and fixed an annoyed look of the more severe variety on me. "*What?*" he asked through tight teeth.

"Just making sure it works," I said, flashing a sweet smile.

When we were out of the little private hallway that came from the wine cellar, the club seemed to thump to life around us. Sensual, porny music was pulsing from a hallway. To complete the picture, a guy was making out with two leather-clad women at the bar.

If only Miss Couch, my second grade teacher, could see me

now. She'd always said how I was such a little sweetheart and how she knew I was going to do something special with my life.

Check it out, Miss C. Little did you know, I would be prowling the underground porn club my grandpa sort of planned to leave me as part of my inheritance.

I jumped when Landon's finger touched my nose. Gently, he tilted my head down, then waited a few seconds to make sure I got the message.

Eyes down. Yeah, yeah.

I tried my best to keep close, but not so close that I got in front of him, but also not so far that people wouldn't think I was "his" while he headed for the bar. It was all so ridiculous. But just like playing with Barbies way, *way* past the appropriate age, there was something fun about knowing I shouldn't be enjoying it.

I sneakily peeked ahead without lifting my head too much and spotted his gloomy black hole of a brother at the bar. A woman was leaning beside him, clearly hoping her massive boobs would get his attention. It appeared they weren't working. I was fairly sure Landon had said his brother ran one of the sister clubs, so I wasn't sure why he always seemed to be here, instead.

Landon put his hand on James' shoulder. "Is she here tonight?"

James turned his head a fraction of an inch toward Landon but didn't look up. "Yes."

God. His voice reminded me of two mountains rubbing together, and not in a sensual kind of way—more like an annoyed shoulder bump while passing in a crowded subway.

"Is who here?" I whispered.

"Wait until you're asked to speak," Landon said under his breath.

As much as I wanted to bite back with an angry reply, I couldn't help feeling the pressure of the club adding weight to his words. It really was like a different world down here. While it irked to have someone actually tell me to "wait until you're asked to speak," it had a different context here. I'd gone to Germany when I was sixteen once, and I pretty quickly learned that nobody over there had discovered carbonated drinks—or drinks in general, taste better with ice. I didn't go around trying to convince the entire country that I was right. I just sucked it up and drank room temperature beverages for two weeks.

As the saying went, when in The Golden Pecker, do as the peckers do. In this case, Landon was the Pecker King. The peckeriest pecker of all, you could say.

So, I batted my eyelashes and studied the floor.

Landon watched me, then nodded. "Come with me. I'm going to show you the sensory deprivation room."

I wanted to ask a question, but I could tell from the look in his eyes that he was waiting for me to slip up again. *Wait until I'm asked to speak.* With an internal sigh, I shoved the question into the back of my mind and followed obediently. I couldn't say why but bowing to his authority filled my lower stomach with a not-so-unpleasant kind of warmth.

I recognized the hallway we moved through, as well as the curtains leading to two of the rooms I'd been in already. My curiosity was piqued by the sheer number of curtained-off areas and then the rows of sturdy looking doors a little farther down the hall. Landon stopped at a door that was painted black. He pulled one of the golden coins from his pocket and slid it into a receptacle below the handle. It reminded me of an arcade machine. There was a little metallic clink, then Landon pushed the door open.

"How do you get your coin back?" I asked.

"Each coin is chipped with an identifier. Some rooms require you to 'spend' your coin for the night. Once it's spent, you can retrieve it on the way out at the reception desk."

I rolled my eyes. "You guys come up with so many overly complicated systems down here. What about just asking for a key like for a gas station bathroom? Hmm? Did anyone consider that before they imbedded microchips inside metal coins?"

Landon gave me a look that said I was walking on thin ice.

I blew out a frustrated breath and made an exaggerated show of redirecting my eyes to the ground and zipping my lips.

The room was nothing but a narrow walkway covered in a soft, black fabric shaped like the inside of an egg carton. The floor below the walkway, the walls, and the ceiling were all clad in those spikey, sound dampening triangles like the kind YouTubers stuck on their walls. As soon as the door closed behind us, the most intense silence I'd ever felt seemed to crush in around me.

"Wow," I said. *"Wow,"* I said again, more quietly. I couldn't quite put my finger on it, but even my voice sounded different—like little echoes and reverberations that normally only registered subconsciously were absent as well.

"It's state of the art sound dampening technology. Almost every surface is covered in it. And that's the tub," he said, gesturing to a little bowl that was surrounded by the same soft, black spikes. I could see now that it was full of water.

"Wait," I said. "I'm supposed to get in that thing? I didn't bring a change of clothes."

"You won't be needing them," Landon said. "And I'm being gentle with you because it's your first night as my submissive, but I expect you to learn without needing to be reminded of the rules again."

I winced. *Right.* I was asking questions again. I clamped my mouth shut.

"Good," he said.

I hated how his praise made a little ball of pride blossom in my chest. I was starting to see how women could get addicted to this, silly or not.

"Take off your dress and get in the tub," he commanded.

I opened my mouth to protest, then remembered the rules. I

closed my eyes, trying to think of a way to ask him to turn off the lights first without getting in trouble.

"Here," he said in a voice that was surprisingly gentle. He took me by the arm and led me to the edge of the tub. "When I turn off the lights, it will be absolutely dark. Not the kind of dark you're used to. I want you to take off your clothes when the lights are off —even your underwear—and hand it to me. Then take my hand and I'll help you get into the tub."

I took a deep breath and studied the vaguely alien ceiling. It really felt like I was losing my mind. I was in this strange, aggressively quiet room. Landon was towering over me like a bossy, mysterious demon, and... *And I was considering stripping completely naked and getting into a bathtub in the secret BDSM club below my grandfather's hotel.*

I closed my eyes, then nodded my head. Giving my assent made my entire body light up. I could feel every hair standing on end and I knew Landon must've heard the impossibly loud thumping of my heart. The room was so quiet, he probably could even hear the blood sloshing around in my veins.

He clapped his hands twice, and the lights cut out.

Despite my best efforts, I laughed out loud. "Clap on, clap off lights? Really?" I asked,

"People kept losing the remote," he muttered.

My smile quickly faded when reality sank in. I was doing this. I really was about to strip naked only inches away from a man who was practically a stranger. The only thing separating my kind of dimpled ass, the unfortunately placed freckle that kind of blurred the border of one of my nipples, and all my other points of self-consciousness from his eyes were two claps of his hands.

I pulled my dress over my head and extended it toward where he'd been standing. I found his hands and passed it to him. Next, I unclasped my bra, and then slid out of my panties. I set both of them on top of the dress and then waited for his hand. He took me by the wrist and guided me into the tub.

The whole experience was already surreal. Once I took my mind off undressing, I realized just how dark the room was. Like the silence, it was another factor beyond *dark*. It felt as if the darkness wasn't just around me or in front of me, but like it had flooded to the inside of my eyes and brain, too. It made me realize how even when I'd been in dark places before, my mind was just working overtime to process what little visual information was available—hints of a wall here or an object there. This darkness was so complete that I could feel a sort of stillness in my brain, like it wasn't even trying.

The unexpected sensation of his hand against me in that dark silence seemed to magnify everything, even the barely audible rasp of his calloused skin against me.

The water sloshed as I slid into the tub. I was pleased to find it wasn't cold at all. In fact, it was as close to a neutral temperature as I thought there could be. It felt like nothing, just like the rest of the room, and I understood now why the tub was the final step of the sensory deprivation.

"No jokes?" Landon asked. His voice seemed to float in the darkness just above me.

I frowned up toward him, even though I couldn't see a thing. I was certainly nervous, but the gravity of the moment was starting to weigh down everything else. I realized I'd been treating this whole thing like I was taking a tour of a chocolate factory. I figured I'd just pop my head in, take a look around, and leave the way I came once I had my fill. Clearly, I'd been very, *very* wrong.

This was the part of the tour where the Oompa Loompas emerged, locked the doors, and started singing. *What do you get when you play with your, heart? You get naked in the, tu-ub!* I was pretty sure that wasn't how the song went, but I was definitely naked and in the tub. I was also neck deep, and I wasn't just talking about the water.

"Relax your head back," Landon said.

I shivered when his fingertips pressed lightly into the sides of my head, easing it back to rest on a small, padded ledge at the back of the tub.

"Good," he said.

Just the sound of his voice alone was so overpowering in the black silence. It sent shivers across my body—or maybe that was his hands on me when I was naked, even if I knew he couldn't see anything.

"Now," Landon said. "Touch yourself for me."

When I didn't move, I felt him kneel until our faces must've only been inches apart. "You remember the safe words, don't you?"

I nodded, stupidly realized he couldn't see me, then whispered a hoarse, *yes.*

"Good. Then I'm only going to say it one more time. Your options are to touch yourself, or I'll do it for you. You have three seconds to choose."

I felt the weight of each passing second like fists to my stomach. *One... Two...*

Almost as if it had a mind of its own, my hand slid up my stomach to cup one of my breasts.

"Tell me what you're doing," Landon said. His voice was a low, raspy whisper. If I didn't know better, I would've said there was a hint of animalistic need in his tone, too.

I bit my lip. "I'm holding my boob."

"Tell me how it feels."

I swallowed, and the sound might as well have been two cymbals crashing together in the silent room. "Good. Better than it should? Like my hand is extra warm, and it's making little tingles go all over my body."

"Put your other hand between your legs."

I let my thumb rub across my hardening nipple and shivered. My other hand moved through the water, gliding across my body in a way that felt far, *far* too sensual to be happening while Landon hovered inches away in the dark.

"This feels so dirty," I said.

"'Dirty' gets a bad reputation. One it doesn't deserve."

I tried to just rest my hand between my legs, but there was an invisible current running through the room—like Landon's commands were strings that led back to an unseen puppeteer who waited somewhere in the shadows of the huge, silent room. I couldn't stop myself from playing along, and everything felt so inexplicably good that I wasn't sure I even wanted to stop anymore.

A moan slipped from my lips. I clamped my mouth shut, but my traitorous hands didn't stop.

"You say it feels dirty," Landon continued in a low, heavy voice. "You're enjoying something, but you're letting society make you feel guilty for it. That's what 'dirty' is. Society isn't here, Andi. It's only me, you, and the darkness. You're just doing as you're told. *Obeying*," he added.

His words sent another wave of heat through me. *Jesus.* I let two of my fingers slide into my entrance as I used the palm of my hand to rub my clit. I liked to think I knew my way around my own body, but nothing I'd ever done—solo or otherwise—held a candle to the way this felt.

And then he touched me.

My body was so overwhelmed that I didn't even recognize what was happening at first. It was just his fingers against my cheek, then his thumb found my lips as he blindly explored. He let his finger stay there, gliding across my lower lip. Instinctively, I tried to lick my dry lips and felt my tongue flick against his finger.

Another, pitiful little gasp escaped me, and before I knew what I was doing, I was kissing his finger. It was slow at first, but I felt so uncontrollably turned on that I couldn't stop myself.

Yellow. Red. The safe words floated into my mind like buoys in the middle of a storm—safe places I could reach out for and find shelter. Instead, I kept kissing his finger, driven boldly forward by the sharp intake of breath I heard from him. It was hot. *God,* it was so unbelievably hot.

I pictured his piercing eyes just inches from mine and wondered about the dark secret I knew he still hid from me. I wondered if this would change anything—if I was really foolish enough to think I could win his trust with my body. But that wasn't even true. Nothing I was doing felt deliberate. It was all natural, like breathing when my lungs burned or trying to paddle if I found myself in the middle of the ocean.

It should have mattered. All of it should have—my questions and my lack of answers. But I was being carried by his momentum, and the current of that power was too strong to fight.

And I could get drunk on that sound I'd heard when I took his finger in my mouth. It said there was a fire of longing inside him, and every movement of my mouth against him was stoking those flames. There was power in that feeling. Intoxicating power.

18

LANDON

SHIT.

I hadn't meant to touch her. The decision had been more of an impulse that happened before I had time to stop it. But once I felt her silky, warm skin, I couldn't help myself. Then I felt her lips...

And now her hot tongue was doing magic with the sensitive pad of my thumb, brushing and teasing. I could feel the wet grip of her lips circling the base of my finger and my already hard dick throbbed when I imagined how it would feel to take her mouth the way I wanted.

Worse, I could hear the gradually increasing pace of her hand churning up the water of the tub. I couldn't see a thing, but I knew what that sound meant. I could picture her delicate fingers sliding into her tight entrance and rubbing hungry circles around her clit. I could see it all so goddamn clearly it hurt.

I needed to take control back. I knew I did. My role as her dom was to be the one in command, even if I had softened the terms of the contract for Andi. I wasn't supposed to let myself get carried away or to let my submissive take control like this. Letting things continue like they were, even for a few more moments, threatened to unravel that delicate balance of power.

And then there was a sound that didn't belong. The lock I'd engaged on the door clicked, then there was the faintest hint of light.

Two loud claps rang out and all the lights in the room exploded to life.

I was already looking toward the source of the sound, so I was able to see the green fingernails and a pair of feminine hands before they slid back out of the door.

Without thinking, I looked back to Andi. *That was a mistake.*

The fraction of a second before she hurried to cover her naked body burned itself immediately into my memory. I could practically feel the edges of the image etching themselves into my brain, burrowing into my subconscious. Perfectly perky nipples on her modestly sized chest—wide hips and a narrow waist... *And her hand.* I could see the two fingers she still had inside her tight, gorgeous entrance.

Within the blink of an eye, one of her arms was covering her nipples and her legs were crossed with the other hand covering as much as it could. I quickly clapped my hands twice, returning us to darkness, but we both knew the damage was already done. Except I was sure she had no idea how much that moment was going to torment me.

My dick was so painfully hard I thought it might burst.

"Here," I said hoarsely. I reached blindly under the tub for the towels I knew were stowed beneath. "Take my hand and I'll help you get dried off."

A wet hand pressed against my face a moment later. One of her fingers slid up my nose. I flinched back, laughing in surprise. "Uh, that was my face."

"Sorry," she said. "I was trying to find your hand. And I guess I hadn't had enough sticking my fingers in holes for one night. *Please tell me I didn't say that out loud,"* she muttered.

I smiled freely because I knew she couldn't see it. I took her hand in mine. It wasn't lost on me that just a few moments ago, the fingers wrapping themselves around mine had been inside her.

I helped her to stand, then somewhat clumsily extended the open towel. She took it from me, then clapped her hands twice. I was surprised to see her standing there with the towel wrapped around herself. Her long legs were still glistening with water, but only the tips of her hair had gotten wet.

She gave me an expectant look, then gestured for me to turn. "I didn't feel like falling off this bridge in the dark while I tried to get dressed. But if you turn around to peek again, I'm going to Sparta your ass into those little black spikey things down there."

I smirked. "They're actually very soft. I think I'd survive."

I could sense her glaring at my back. "Don't you dare peek."

I already saw enough to ruin me. Don't worry. "I won't."

"Was that part of the experience?" she asked.

I heard the towel drop to the ground. My stomach clenched. All I'd need to do was turn around and that intoxicating body would be right there for the taking.

"No," I said. "I have a feeling I know who that was, and *why*. Planning that would've been a violation. It's not something I would've done to you. *Ever*."

"Because you didn't want to see me naked, you mean?"

I took some time to formulate my answer. Her tone was unreadable. I couldn't tell if she was playfully searching for some validation, or if she was mad and the anger was just now setting in. I wouldn't have blamed her for either.

"Because you wouldn't have had a chance to safe word out of that situation," I said. "I don't want to blindly force you into uncomfortable situations. I want your submission. I want you to know what's coming and then agree to participate."

"I see," she said. "You can turn now."

I was relieved to see she was fully dressed again. Even though my cock still felt like an over-filled balloon about to pop at any moment, I could at least regain some semblance of control.

"Do I get credit for that on the list?" Andi asked.

I couldn't be sure, but I thought she was probably forcing her casual tone. Her chest was still rising and falling a little too fast and I didn't think I'd seen her blink yet.

"Yes," I said. *Take back control, Landon.* "I'll walk you out. But you need work on being a submissive before I can say you actually checked that one off." I paused to search for the right words. As much as I didn't want to offer her an out, I knew it was the least I could do, considering I was still too much of a coward to come clean about everything. "I meant what I said, Andi. Whether you do the list or not, I won't keep your share of the hotel."

She met my eyes, not speaking at first. "I know," she said finally.

Andi was silent as she followed me out of the room, but I could imagine how her thoughts must be racing. I had to admit I enjoyed pushing *her* buttons for a change. In fact, if I was being entirely honest, I enjoyed quite a lot about spending time with her.

Grant practically ran into me once we left the sensory deprivation room. He was out of breath.

"I thought you left hours ago," I said.

Grant shrugged. "Yeah, well, I had a few too many free drinks on you and wound up passed out in the bathroom. Sue me. But you know who is here, and she has been asking for you. Looks like she's out for blood. I'd—"

"You can tell me about it later." I tried to push past him, but he stopped me with a hand on my shoulder.

"This is one of those problems you can't save for later. You know, like that time I realized I'd accidentally stolen that guy's car? Remember? It was push-to-start and he left his keys in it, so it just kinda kicked on. I was halfway home before I—"

"I remember," I growled. "I'm going to walk Andi out of the club, and then I'll deal with your little problem."

"It's actually *your* problem. And it's not so little."

"I can walk myself out," Andi said.

I turned and shot her a warning look. I was somewhat surprised when she lowered her eyes. Submissive wasn't an adjective I'd have used to describe Andi at any point since meeting her, but it was good to see she could learn. I had no doubt she was thinking something sarcastic and biting, but at least she had the self-control to play along. Later, I'd learn her cues well enough to punish her when I sensed her rebellious thoughts, but—

No. There wasn't going to be a later. Andi wasn't *really* my submissive. We were still letting William's list lead us along. Maybe she was playing along for now, but sooner or later, she'd be done with the game.

I took her by the hand and half-dragged her toward the hallway leading to the wine cellar exit.

We drew more than a few stares when we reached the bar area, and I didn't need to be a detective to sense that something was going on. Sydney was wearing a devious smile when she spotted us. She set her drink down and headed straight our way.

My chest went tight. "Ignore her."

"Who is that?" Andi asked.

"I'm Landon's ex-girlfriend," Sydney said.

Even if Andi was making me look like the dom who couldn't control his sub in front of the entire club, I was proud to see that she didn't shrink from Sydney in the slightest.

"Sydney," I said. "Fuck. Off. I'm going to walk Andi out, then I'll deal with you."

Sydney pursed her lips. "What's the harm in letting me talk to your latest toy? Or are you scared she won't play anymore if she knows the truth about you?"

"And what truth is that?" Andi asked.

"Enough," I said. "I'll tell her myself."

Sydney frowned. "Tell her *what*?"

"Not here."

"What is going on?" Andi demanded.

I took her by the hand and tried to lead her out. Andi planted her feet. "By the way," she said to Sydney. "Nice fingernails. Green to symbolize that you're a jealous bitch, or is it just your favorite color?"

Andi had noticed, too. Sydney was the one who turned the lights on, but if she thought she was going to put distance between us with that little stunt, she'd been wrong. Seeing Andi... *No*, that was an image that could drive a man insane with need. Even my imagination hadn't done her justice. But I had a feeling when I finished coming clean to Andi, that snapshot was going to be my parting gift.

Sydney sneered. "Jealous? Landon uses people up and tosses them out when he's done. I was smart enough to leave before he got the chance."

Andi looked at me with fire in her eyes. "Is it against club rules or something if I punch her in the throat?"

I pushed down the urge to smile. "As much as I'd enjoy watching that. *Yes*. It would technically fall under an act of nonconsensual punishment." I knew I'd probably pay for it later, but Andi wasn't budging from my gentle tugs on her hand, so I scooped her up like a child and carried her toward the wine cellar exit.

A low murmur erupted in our wake, but I tried not to hear it. I also tried not to think what it implied about my shaky status as the one in charge of The Golden Pecker. I was losing control, little by little. I knew that much. Showing myself in front of the members with a submissive who was anything but submissive wasn't going to help ease their minds, either. They thought I was grooming her to take over the club, and they no doubt expected her to run the place into the ground with her inexperience.

Andi at least waited until we were out of view from the crowded lobby to start punching my chest. When I ignored the first few comically soft punches, she dipped her index finger in her mouth and then stuck it in my ear. I nearly dropped her with surprise.

"What the hell?" I said, setting her down, but being careful not to let her try to rush past me toward the lobby.

She stuck a finger in my chest. "In a second, I'm going to give you a piece of my mind for embarrassing me like that. But first. *Wow*. You made picking me up look so easy. For somebody who was feeling self-conscious about a few chocolate-induced pounds I've gained over the past couple weeks, that was great for my self-esteem. *No. Don't smile,"* she snapped, jabbing her finger into my chest again. "Because that was also a total dick move. That Sydney woman is going to think she can walk all over me now. You know, I was bullied in high school, and one thing I learned was that it's just like prison. The first day you get bullied, you've got to punch somebody so hard in the face that everybody else gets the message. But instead of punching her in the face, I got carried out of there like a baby."

"You're right, and you're wrong."

She frowned. "Pretty sure you have to pick one of those."

"I shouldn't have picked you up. But I needed to get you out of there because I wanted you to hear the truth from me. Not Sydney."

"What truth?" she asked.

"I should've told you right away, but I—" I closed my eyes. Don't make excuses for yourself. Just lay it out there and let her decide if she ever wants to speak to you again. "William was my biological father. When he and my mother divorced, I took her last name."

Andi stared, then smiled. "That doesn't make any sense."

"When he took you and your sisters in, he and my mom had been divorced about three years. Running the clubs for him was the only reason James and I saw him anymore. My mom cheated on him, and when James and I weren't willing to cut mom out of our lives, he saw it as a betrayal. He started drinking more. I think he only kept us in his lives with the club as a way to punish us."

Andi was shaking her head now, her smile all but faded. "How does giving you a cushy job count as punishment?" she laughed suddenly. "No. I really can't believe any of this."

"He just paid us enough to get by but strung us along on the idea that we'd inherit the club one day. I guess we thought he'd get over his anger about mom eventually, and things would get better. But then he adopted you guys and it was like a switch flipped. You three were—"

Andi shook her head more fiercely, pursing her lips. "No. You know what? Either you're telling the truth and you're an asshole for hiding this, or you're lying and you're an asshole for making up such a shitty story. All I know is I'm tired of looking at your face, and I hope I never have to see it again."

I wanted to reach for her and stop her from going, but I knew I deserved every bit of her anger. I'd been an idiot to wait so long to tell her the truth. If I'd gotten it in the open sooner, it would have been uncomfortable, but nothing we couldn't overcome.

I needed to let her go. I knew one thing. I could still give her the hotel. I didn't expect to earn her forgiveness, but I wanted to at least do one thing right in this mess. I owed her that much.

19

ANDI

I wanted to cry and yell at the same time. In a few seconds, Landon had upended my reality on two fronts. I wanted to think he was lying, but something in my gut told me it was all true.

Grandpa was Landon's father.

I felt an uncomfortable chill run through me. It was weird enough when grandpa had compelled me into a sexual to-do list with a stranger. Knowing that stranger was his *son* made it about a thousand times creepier.

Even though I fully planned to cut Landon out of my life entirely, I tried to smooth over the emotional scarring. For starters, grandpa wasn't *really* my grandpa. He had also never fully taken on a father-like role for us. Instead, he was like a mentor and an adult figure who kept a roof over our heads. And Landon was more like his ex-son, somehow.

I got back to my room and flopped down on the bed, staring at the ceiling. It was still weird. If I wasn't so pissed and confused, I'd probably waste more time trying to decide if a hypothetical relationship between an estranged son and his dad's adopted daughter was taboo. Instead, I just wanted to punch Landon in his stupid face.

God.

Why had he waited so long to tell me the truth? He had let me do all those things with him while *he* knew exactly who he was. He'd made the decision for me, and I thought I might always hate him for that.

My thoughts turned back to Grandpa Willy. The new information about Landon put the video and the list into a new light, and I thought I was starting to see how the pieces fit together.

Maybe he had always intended to try to set us up? No, that didn't make sense. But it might have been an idea that came to him near the end—like a dying wish. Or maybe he thought it would somehow redeem him if he could connect the son he'd screwed up raising with the adoptive daughter he felt he'd done a better job with?

I decided I didn't care anymore. It was going to take time to repair my idea of Grandpa Willy, and I didn't think there was enough time in the world to repair my feelings for Landon.

Bree let herself into my room a few hours later. She found me eating a room service cheeseburger and fries on the bed. I was watching some cheesy horror movie about a basketball that came to life and terrorized a small town.

Bree surveyed the situation, then sat down with a serious expression on her face beside my bed. "Want to talk about it?"

"Well," I said. "I'm pretty sure this guy—he's like the star basketball player for the high school team—is going to end up shooting the death ball through some kind of hoop and ripping an epically corny line to wrap this thing up. I was thinking, '*lay down.*' You know? Like a play on a layup."

Bree squinted one eye and raised her other eyebrow. "I was talking about this." She gestured to my mini feast on the bed.

"Got hungry," I said, popping a fry into my mouth.

"What happened?"

I let out an annoyed sigh. As much as Audria could irritate me with her clinical coldness, Bree was worse. Trying to hide something from her was about as fruitless as trying to convince a dog that bacon wasn't cooking in the kitchen. I paused the movie and spent the next few minutes explaining most of what had happened, minus the awkward sexual bits.

Bree was frowning when I'd finished. "And you believe all of this?" she asked. "About grandpa, I mean."

"It kind of makes sense. I mean, he never talked about his past or ex-wives or anything, but didn't you always kind of feel like he'd led a different life before us?"

"Yeah," Bree said. "Maybe. Does Audria know?"

"No. I went straight for room service. I've been punishing this hamburger and fries. That's it."

Bree worked her lips to the side. "Want me to tell her?"

"No, it's okay. I feel like this is all my mess, somehow."

"Well, I have some good news," Bree said. "I actually stopped by to remind you about Dana's wedding. With everything going on, I kind of figured you forgot. *Annnd* judging by the look on your face, I was correct."

I grinned. "Yeah. Totally forgot."

"Well, she sent us tickets to Florida yesterday. I was thinking you, me, and Audria could go get our dresses tomorrow."

"A few hundred miles between me and Landon sounds perfect. Sign me up."

"You're already kind of signed up," Bree said.

I sighed. "It's a figure of speech. I'm just saying I'm in."

I SPENT THE TWO DAYS AFTER MY NAKED ENCOUNTER IN THE SENSORY deprivation tub aggressively avoiding Landon, fiddling with some writing projects, and catching up on some Netflix. I'd been wrong about the high school basketball star's corny line, too. He had said, 'nothing but dead,' which was a completely lame play on "nothing but net," when he shot the death ball into a trash compactor.

Putting two days between Landon's big reveal had only made me feel more confused. There was a small, *small,* part of me that felt sorry for him. That part of me could kind of understand how awkward it was to explain the truth to me. But the rest of me was still firmly of the belief that he'd knowingly deceived me and hid the truth for way too long. The bottom line was I couldn't trust him, and that was enough to convince me to end the little BDSM experiment, along with any hopes of claiming my share of the inheritance.

Landon had admitted he planned to give me the share of the hotel whether I finished his list or not, but somehow, I suspected that promise only held when he thought he had a shot with me romantically. Now that I was firmly out of the picture, I didn't doubt he'd change his mind.

If nothing else, I knew I was going to be stuck in Florida for a week. That meant even if I had ill-advised urges to give him a second chance, I'd be too far away to act on them. It was an opportunity to let all the chemicals in my system flush out, along with the raging hormones he seemed to cause.

I sat between Bree and Audria on the plane, and we'd just hit that point where my ears felt like they flooded with wet cotton. I wiggled in my seat in discomfort, then tried to yawn a couple times to no avail.

Bree was wearing a gigantic black hoodie, which was so far from her normal style that I wanted to laugh out loud every time I looked at her. The sleeves were so big and baggy that she kept having to hold her arms in the air and wiggle them to free her hands.

"Are you going to tell me what the deal is with your hoodie, or do I have to ask?" I said.

She pulled the hood over her head, pretending not to hear.

I yanked her earbuds out and leaned forward, forcing her to

acknowledge me. "Tell me, or I'll tickle it out of you, right here on this plane in front of everybody. *And you know what happened last time I tickled you in public.*"

That got her attention. "It's a friend's hoodie. He wanted me to have it for the trip since he was worried I'd miss him."

I leaned in and sniffed it. "Ahh, yes. I can smell the teenage boy lust all over it. A *friend*, huh? Is he cute?"

"He is cute, but it's not like that. He's just... Complicated. Okay?"

Normally, I would've officially begun the interrogation and dug out every last detail. Instead, the word *complicated* only called up an image of Landon's face. No matter how much annoyance and anger was tangled up with that image, it still made something in my chest feel heavy. *Definitely not my heart.* It was probably a lung, or something.

"Woah," Bree said. As usual, she was frustratingly perceptive. "Not like you to leave low hanging fruit without at least taking a swing."

I shrugged. "Sorry. I just couldn't decide between saying nothing was complicated about giving blowjobs when micropenises are involved or that this guy was absolutely stalking your social accounts by now."

"*One.* I didn't need to know about your extensive experience with micropenises. *Two.* He's just a friend. Seriously."

Audria leaned over. "Then why did he practically give that hoodie a bath in his cologne? He's clearly trying to psychologically program you. He wants you to associate that smell with the great time you're going to have at the wedding. When you get back, you'll see him and *bam.* For some reason the overpowering aroma of his cologne is going to make you feel attracted to him."

Bree rolled her eyes.

"She's not entirely wrong," I said. "Classical conditioning. If you pair two stimuli together enough times, our brains make associations between them."

"I know all about Pavlov's dogs," Bree said with the stuffy, know-it-all tone teenagers were masters of. "Apparently, Grandpa Willy did, too."

"Wait," I said. "What is that supposed to mean?"

"Just that it would've been a miracle if you didn't classically condition yourself to have some good feelings when you see Landon by the time you finish that list. I mean, come on. He was obviously trying to set you two up."

"That's stupid," I said.

"Also gross," Audria added. "Landon is practically her stepbrother, if what he said is true."

"Now hold on," I said. "I don't think that's really true. If your adoptive grandfather had a son, he'd be more like..."

Bree made a barfing gesture. "Yeah. He's more like your stepdad."

Both her and Audria started cracking up.

"*Stop,*" I said, covering my face and laughing. "Technically, it wouldn't be anything. We were adopted, not married into a family. Either way, I'm over him now so it's irrelevant."

Bree squinted. "Are you though? You were pretty ready to run away. People usually only run from things they're scared of. And me? I think you're scared you'll take him back."

Audria nodded wisely. "The old siren call of the cock. It's deadly, I hear."

I gave them both an unamused look. "Believe it or not, my attraction to him died with my trust. So, *no.* There's no siren call."

Bree blew a raspberry. "Bull. A guy like that could read you passages from the encyclopedia and it'd be erotic." She dipped her chin and did her best impression of Landon's deep, gruff voice. "And the male hummingbird slides his beak into the flower's narrow entrance. If he can't siphon its precious juices, he won't have the energy to find another. His life quite literally depends on getting his beak wet."

I shook my head, laughing sourly. "I'm just planning to enjoy this wedding. It'll give me a few days away from Landon and the stupid list. Who knows, maybe I'll even meet somebody new to take my mind off of him."

"Right," Audria said. "Because you're totally the type of person to hook up with random guys on a trip."

"And," Bree said. "You're not exactly prime real estate right now if you think about it. I mean, what kind of new boyfriend wants to find out his woman is working on a BDSM to-do list with Mr. Supermodel?"

"*Was working*," I corrected. "But you guys are right, anyway. I'm hardly a dick magnet, so it's not like it matters. What's important is just getting some time away from everything so I can think straight for once."

Bree gave my leg a comforting squeeze. "Don't worry, Andi. Nobody is a dick magnet. They're not metallic, so it's basically impossible."

I grinned. "Unless they are heavily pierced."

She made a face. "Gross."

Audria nodded, as if she had some experience on the topic. "Everybody thinks dick piercings are cool until they come loose and get lodged up your cooch."

"Wow," I said, sticking earbuds in and turning on some music. "What a great time to end the conversation."

20

LANDON

James and Grant were standing inside my office—James with his arms crossed broodingly by the door and Grant doing some kind of yoga stretch against the wall.

"Could you focus, please?" I asked Grant.

He turned his head to look at me but was still digging his palm into the small of his back as he tried to arch himself into the shape of a "C". He groaned in satisfaction. "There it is." He straightened, rolled his neck, and raised his eyebrows. "I can focus better when I don't have a tight back."

"People in the club are talking," I said. "After the little show down by the bar, they are convinced Andi is going to inherit the club."

"So, go to the lawyers," Grant suggested. "Claim that shit. If your conscience is a problem, just sort it out later. Once it's in your name, it's still your call. What difference does it make if she gets the club from the lawyers, or from you?"

James pulled a disgusted face. "You're not seriously considering giving her the club." It wasn't even a question. It was a statement, like the idea was so idiotic he didn't even need to ask.

I shrugged, glaring. "I don't know what I'm considering. I just wish I had more time to think."

"Yeah," Grant said. "But you don't. And unlike you, I don't need days to figure out something as obvious as grilled cheese and ketchup. Go to the lawyers. Say she bailed on the list. Get your papers, and then you can at least put a pause to the rumors. Show anyone who cares your goddamn name on the title for this place."

I scratched at the stubble on my chin in irritation. What he was saying made sense, but it didn't feel right. It would be yet another move to undermine Andi's trust. And if I hadn't already shattered the last hope of fixing things with her, it seemed like finding out I'd gone ahead and stolen her inheritance would.

"He's thinking about doing something stupid," James said in a bored voice.

Grant squinted. "Yep. Definitely."

"There's something I need to handle first."

"Think Sydney and Edward are fucking?" James asked offhandedly.

"Ohh," Grant said. "Twisty. I like that. Think they're fucking? *Nah.* Sydney's not the type to join a harem. She's freaky, but more in a lick your asshole kind of way."

I stared. "How would you know?"

Grant held his hands up. "People tell me things, man. Something about my wise eyes or my friendly disposition, I guess."

"Yeah, I'm sure that's it," I said dryly.

"How bad is the affliction?" Grant asked.

"What?" I asked.

"These feelings you have for Andi. It has clearly passed beyond the point of logic, or you wouldn't be making so many stupid decisions for her sake."

"Yeah, I have feelings for Andi," I said. "This would be a lot easier if I didn't."

"I hate to break it to you," Grant said. "But the situation

between you and that girl is a recipe for disaster. I mean, you're basically one step removed from being the guy who took her hostage. Not only that, you're *sort of* compelling her toward sexual acts with you. You also lied about who you were from the get-go. I mean, if that doesn't round you out to being the last man on earth she'd develop feelings for, I don't know what does."

I'd never admit as much out loud, but Grant had a point. Several, in fact. While I didn't sign up for this, I also hadn't done anything to stop it from happening. I could've refused my inheritance or agreed to pass it back to her. I could've done plenty to avoid how things had played out. Instead, I'd only selfishly focused on my own best interests. I didn't care if I made some spoiled granddaughter of a wealthy old man uncomfortable. Admittedly, I'd figured she'd run after the first night.

"What about the wedding?" Grant said.

"What wedding?"

"The one Andi left for this morning."

I stared. "She left?"

"Damn," Grant said. "Your stalking skills are so weak. It's pathetic. But yes, the woman getting married is the daughter of some rich asshole who was close to William. The wedding is going to be in Florida."

"You want him to crash the wedding?" James asked. "To what end?"

Grant shrugged. "Keep tabs on this woman he has the hots for? I mean, obviously he's doomed, but he at least can have a front row seat to his own gory end, right?"

My mind was on Andi and what she might do to vent her anger with me. I thought of her finding some other guy—some person she might sleep with to get me out of her system.

The idea made me clench my teeth so hard it hurt. "Going to the wedding wouldn't be the dumbest idea you've ever had, Grant."

"No," James said. "But that's not saying much."

"He makes jokes now?" Grant asked, jabbing a thumb toward James. "Guess what, you big, creepy asshole? Your jokes suck. You should stick to being a weird, grouchy statue. It suits you better."

James turned to face Grant, who wasn't short by any standards at a few inches over six feet, but he still seemed small beside James. To his credit, Grant stared up into James' eyes and didn't flinch back.

"Come on. Nobody needs to fight," I said. "Grant, your plan was good. James, you really aren't funny. Case closed."

"Well," Grant said. "What are you going to do?"

"What do you think?" I asked, grabbing my coat and standing.

21

ANDI

Dana Whitmoore and I used to be really close. We went to the same high school and her father was friends with Grandpa Willy. But after high school, our lives went in completely different directions. She took over an important job in her father's business and became ultra-successful in her own right. Now she was marrying a guy I didn't know named Jim.

One thing was immediately evident when we arrived in St. Augustine, Florida, for the wedding. Money was not in short supply. Everybody who was invited had their plane tickets covered and a free room in this sprawling, beautiful old historic hotel. It was nestled in the shade of massive, oak trees and surrounded by green grass in every direction.

My sisters and I took rooms on the top floor, which we selected after taking an hour-long tour of the building. I could've believed I had been transported back to the 1700s when I was in the place. Every scrap of furniture looked antique, but stunningly preserved. The paintings on the walls were all regal and proud depictions of some ancient family line.

I flopped down on the four-poster bed in my room and sighed contentedly. This was exactly what I needed. *Space.*

I could hear Bree and Audria in the rooms on either side of mine as they unpacked their things, but it was still a different kind of quiet out here. After spending most of my life in New York City, I had stopped noticing the background noise a long time ago. I closed my eyes and drank in the silence that seemed to envelop this place like a comfortable little cocoon, but then my mind went somewhere dangerous.

I remembered the dark room and the sensation of feeling nothing as I floated in the tub. I remembered how my skin had tingled with the knowledge that Landon was so close. And I remembered his hands on my face—his thumb against my lips.

My door opened and a guy came halfway in with a bag over his shoulder.

I shot up on the bed, eyes wide and breathless.

"Oh, shit," he said. "Sorry—I didn't realize someone was in here. I was trying to find my room."

I squinted. I recognized him. It had been several years since I'd seen him, and he'd put on muscle in the right places and grown up since then. "Tommy?"

He pointed, nodding with a friendly smile. "Andi. Right? Shit, yeah. That's you for sure."

I was more than a little startled when he dropped his bag and walked over to me for a hug. I was still sitting on the bed when he wrapped his arms around me.

He pulled back from the hug, smiling like he had no idea why it could be inappropriate to hug me while I was sitting on a bed. I wasn't sure if I was the one reading too much into it, though, so I smiled like nothing was weird, too. "Do you still drum your fingers on everything within reach?" I asked. I tried to stand, which meant awkwardly slinking around him since he was still standing right in front of me.

"Actually, I use drumsticks most of the time now. I made a career out of it. I do recording gigs for big bands. Some of the really big ones, actually."

"Oh, wow," I said. I was still smiling, but I felt like a deer in the headlights. I didn't think it had anything to do with the fact that Tommy Gallager from high school had grown up to be certifiably hot. I remembered his mom was actually from Okinawa, Japan, and his dad was Italian. The mixed heritage suited him well, but that wasn't what had me feeling so nervous and awkward. It was the thought of Landon finding out.

Just the thought of Landon irritated me. He didn't deserve to be on my mind, just like he didn't deserve to ruin this trip.

"You good?" he asked. "Shit," he laughed at himself and walked to my door, where he casually rested a hand on the frame and smiled. "Maybe if I didn't barge into your personal space next time, huh?"

"No, it's totally fine," I said quickly. I followed him to the door and tried to stop acting like such a social virgin. I scrambled to think of a believable lie to explain why I was acting so weird. "I actually just finished this TV series I was super into. So I'm kind of in that... post show depression. *Yeah.*"

Tommy nodded like he actually knew what I was talking about. "Been there. When *Dexter* finished, I felt like a part of me died with it. Or maybe it was just the shitty finale?" He chuckled softly at himself. "But, hey. The best thing to get you over it is a rebound."

I felt my eyes go wide. *Did he seriously just proposition me for sex?* "I don't know if—I mean, that's not—"

"A rebound show," he said slowly. "I've been to weddings like this before. We're going to have a ton of downtime. What do you say we meet up somewhere and I can introduce you to a new show? There's just a little informal "welcome" dinner tonight, and then we could hang out after in my room or your room."

"Uh," I stammered.

"Actually, your room has a massive TV, wow," he said, pointing to the wall. "Kind of doesn't fit the whole ancient history aesthetic, but I'm not complaining. Let's do your room then.

Catch you after the party?" He drummed his fingers on the door-frame and took a step back, pointing expectantly at me.

Feeling overwhelmed and bombarded, all I did was shrug and raise my eyebrows.

Tommy nodded, gave a little wave, and walked off.

As soon as he was around the corner, Audria and Bree both burst out of their rooms.

"Eavesdropping? Seriously?" I asked.

"Uh, I, uh, er, uh," Audria mimicked. "If that little routine from you led to him asking you to hang out, he's *really* desperate. You know that, right?"

"Yeah," Bree agreed. "No offense, but you weren't exactly *'spitting game'* as the kids say."

I rolled my eyes at her. "You are the kids, Bree. And I wasn't trying to get him to ask me to hang out. I was trying to get him out of my room."

"Ah," Audria said. "So, you wanted to get him out of your room, and your best plan was to agree to invite him back to your room tonight after the welcome dinner. *Got it.*"

"There was no plan," I said. *And now I'm feeling all confusingly guilty because this feels like going behind Landon's back somehow.* Except I should actually feel the glorious, red, white, and blue glow of righteous justice for doing exactly that. Hell, I could probably go on a wild sex spree and still not pay him back for hiding such a huge lie. "And maybe the two of you should get a life so you can stop butting into mine."

"As soon as your life stops talking at the top of its lungs outside our rooms, maybe we will," Audria said.

I gestured to the otherwise empty hallway and gave my sisters my best *get a life* glare. Thankfully, they took the hint and left me by myself again. Except that only meant I had a few hours before the welcome dinner to sit and torture myself by mentally running through everything that just happened. I'd agreed to pseudo-date an old high school friend. Meanwhile, I was tangled in a kind of sort of dominant submissive relationship with a guy who looked like a Calvin Klein model back home. *Oh,* and I was regularly having very, very dirty dreams about said guy back home. The fact that I was trying my best to be appropriately mad over what he'd hidden from me was doing depressingly little to stop any of it.

I was also pretty sure Landon would lose his shit if he somehow figured out what was going on. But screw Landon —*just,* well, not in the way I'd been screwing him in my dreams almost every night. He could get figuratively screwed, right along with his over-confident assumption that I'd submit to him.

I HAD A BAD HABIT OF OVER-INDULGING WHEN FREE STUFF WAS involved. For starters, I was the bane of every free sample person's existence. I'd shamelessly stand there and fill up until they were either out of samples or they called security. So when waitstaff started circulating the welcome party to Dana Whitmoore's extravagant, super fancy wedding, I helped myself to everything they were offering.

That meant I'd eaten my weight in little squares of cheese, flaky pastries filled with spinach and cream, crunchy wonton's loaded with crab meat, and my favorite—doughnuts. Yes, among all the fancy, hoity toity options, there was literally a server walking around with a tray of straight-up doughnuts. After a few minutes, they started passing out champagne glasses as well.

Like a medieval king who just gorged on several platters of chicken legs to the point where he could no longer move, I perched in a chair and groggily said my "hello" to old acquaintances and friends who passed by me.

Audria found me about two hours later and shook her head. "You are so ridiculous. It literally looks like you're pregnant right now. How much did you eat?"

I waved my hand. Truth be told, I was a little drunk, despite all the food weighing me down like a delicious little anchor. "Enough."

She laughed. "You're going to be a real catch for your date tonight, assuming his line is strong enough to pull in a blue whale."

I lifted my arm to point warningly at her but lost my balance in the chair and slumped over. I let out a defeated sigh. "As soon as I'm mobile again. I'm going to get you for that."

"This looks a little self-destructive, even by your standards. Is this about Landon?"

I looked her in the eyes and shook my head. "If Landon saw me right now, I'd tell him to suck on a bone."

Audria watched me with raised eyebrows. "I don't know what that means. Is that a sexual thing, or..."

"It's dangerous. Chicken bones splinter and can cut up your insides. So, I'd be telling him to do something dangerous. Because screw him."

"Right. That sounds super dangerous. *If he was a dog.* You might as well tell him to go swimming right after he eats because you hope he gets a cramp and maybe drowns."

"Okay. I'd tell him to pull the pin on a grenade and shove it up his ass, how about that?"

"That's great, but I'm pretty sure you can't just go buy a grenade from Wal Mart. You've got to have some kind of military license and so on."

I narrowed my eyes. "I'm way too drunk and stuffed to be having this conversation right now."

Tommy made his way through the crowd from behind Audria. I inwardly cringed a little. I felt like Jabba The Hut right now. *Meesa made a mistake.* "Hey, Tommy," I said. "Did you try the appetizers?"

"Andi did," Audria said. "All of them. Like six times. I'm sure she can give you some suggestions if you're wondering about any of them."

Tommy smiled. "You look a little wiped out. Want to get out of here?"

Audria gave him a look. "I think she's a little too far gone to go somewhere alone right now, actually."

"Oh, no. Not alone. I mean you can come, too. Assuming you are as over this party as I am."

"Unless you have a wheelbarrow," I said. "I don't think I'm moving. Or one of those mobile, electric scooters like they have at grocery stores. *Whirrrr*," I said, chuckling and holding my hands up to pantomime scootering out of there.

I knew I'd gone overboard on the drinks, but I didn't realize by how much until it felt like somebody started skipping pages on my night. One minute, I was making an idiot out of myself in front of Tommy and my sister. The next, both of them were hauling me back to my room. Then we were watching a movie. Then Audria was sleeping on the bed with me and Tommy was dozing on the couch. After that, I didn't remember anything.

By morning, I thought my head was going to split itself open. I sat up in bed, wincing and pinching my temples. Audria stirred beside me.

She groaned and threaded her fingers together above her head. Her hair was a dark, tangled mess. "Do you still need a babysitter, or can I go to my own room now? I was hoping to get some work done on my thesis before the wedding."

I looked past her to the couch, where Tommy was still asleep. I felt bad for him. He might have been a little aggressively outgoing for my tastes, but I had to admit he was a nice guy. Sweet, even. I'd also hardly given him a chance yet. We had our awkward introductions in my room last night, and the next thing I saw of him, I was drunk out of my mind. "Thank you for staying with me," I said. "But I'm fine now. Just a hangover the size of Schwarzenegger."

She gave me a mock salute, got out of bed, and quietly slipped out of my room. I scooted back and sat up against the headboard, trying to decide where I wanted to go from here. For all I knew, Tommy was going to wake up and try to find his way out of my life as soon as possible.

Images of Landon flashed in my mind. Dark images. I saw him with the shadows from the club playing across his cruelly perfect features. I felt his hot breath between my legs in the locker room of the aquarium and I remembered the taste of his thumb between my lips. Like usual, my body reacted to the memories. My stomach flooded with heat and I had to press my thighs together to fight the hungry pulsing between my legs.

Tommy sat up, and I suddenly felt ten times dirtier. I was lying in bed, probably already soaked, and there was a guy on my couch. Meanwhile, I still hadn't even decided if it was possible to cheat on a guy you kind of sort of had a contractual relationship with—a guy you also had a very good reason to cut out of your life for good.

"Oh, hey," I said. "Looks like you found a wheelbarrow, after all."

He smiled. It was a kind smile. From looking at his face, I thought I could see it all as plain as day. The difference between a guy like Tommy and a guy like Landon was simple: the Tommys of the world were the ones who'd remember your birthday and take you to nice Italian restaurants for Valentine's day. They'd take selfies with you and post them on social media with cute captions, like, "Can't believe she's mine!". Tommy was probably the kind of guy I could have been perfectly happy with. But it felt like I could see all that unroll out into infinity just from a glance at his smile. It was clear. Obvious, even.

Then there was Landon. I wasn't even sure if I could say he was like the Landons of the world, because I suspected he was one of a kind. The future with him might as well have been a closed door. Hell, there was probably smoke billowing out from under the door, too. Maybe even an ominous, red glow. If there were any social media captions from Landon, they'd probably be weird and kinky, like, "This one is mine."

I grinned a little at the thought. Landon did have quite the possessive streak. Normally, that would've put me off. Oddly enough, I found I had enjoyed when I could see him getting jealous of me. I needed to stop thinking of him in the present tense. Somebody who could lie about something like that could lie about all sorts of things.

A smart person would've pursued Tommy a hundred times out of a hundred. But I wasn't sure I wanted to know how everything was going to play out. I wasn't ready to sign up for that—for white picket fences, kids, and flour-coated aprons. It didn't mean I was going to forgive Landon, but just because Landon had screwed up, it also didn't mean I had to rebound into the first guy who showed up.

"Actually," Tommy said. "I'm not sure how much you remember, but your sister and I just kind of half-carried you back here. I have to say, I've never heard a sloppy drunk person sing so well, though. I mean, you butchered the words to "The Eye of the Tiger" and "Macho Man," but it was all perfectly in pitch."

"BS," I said. "I know those songs like the back of my hand. I'd never screw up the lyrics."

We both smiled, and there it was again. I could feel how easy it would be. I just had to keep being myself—to let things play out like they wanted to. He was an attractive guy who was interested in me. He had a respectable job. He was nice. He didn't glare at me like he'd just hopped off the elevator from hell a few minutes ago. *And he didn't make me squirm with need every time he popped into my head.*

I heard Bree outside my door. Tommy and I turned toward the sound, listening intently. She sounded a little scared.

"...not a good idea. Uh, Audria! A little help!"

Somebody tried the handle of my door. Then there were

three loud bangs. "Andi?" A deep voice called. "Open the fucking door."

My eyes went wide. I knew that voice. It was the same voice that had told me to strip out of my clothes. To touch myself.

Without thinking, I threw the covers over my head.

"Andi?" Tommy asked quietly. "Who is that?"

"Shh!" I hissed. "Hide!"

"What the hell?" he asked. "I'm not going to hide."

I heard him walking across the room. Then the door opened.

"Who are you?" Landon demanded.

"Tommy. What do you want?"

"I want you to get out of my fucking way so I can find Andi."

There was an uncomfortable pause.

"I can see you under the blanket, Andi," Landon said.

I slid the blanket down and gave a sheepish little wave. When I saw the look on Landon's face, I realized being buried in the covers of my bed while Tommy was in my room sent the wrong message.

Landon looked like a bull who had seen red. His focus turned to Tommy, and he started advancing with murder in his eyes.

22

LANDON

He was a relatively big guy, but I was pissed enough that it didn't matter. I lifted him by his shirt and slammed him into the nearest wall. I'd pulled my hand back to punch him when something small latched onto my bicep. I looked back and saw Andi tugging on my arm with both her hands. Even as pissed as I was, I didn't fail to notice that she was fully dressed, and judging by the wrinkles in her clothes, she hadn't changed since last night.

My suspicion that she'd slept with this guy dropped from highly probably to less likely, which helped keep me from punching him.

But while I was looking at Andi, the guy I was pinning took his opportunity to punch *me*.

I staggered back from the surprise of it. When I turned to face him, his hands were up like he was ready to fight.

"I have no idea who you are," he said. "But I'm not going to let you hurt Andi."

I wanted to laugh. "Hurt Andi? The only one I'm considering hurting is you."

His hands dropped slightly. He looked at Andi, then me, and

understanding settled on him. "Wait. Are you two together?" He was asking Andi—not me.

We both spoke at the same time, only I said "yes," and she said "no."

"Just stop trying to hit each other," Andi pleaded.

"Is this why you snuck off to Florida?" I asked her. "To fuck this guy who can barely throw a punch?"

"That was a warning shot," the other guy said.

"Great. I'll add child-like tendencies to the long list of your charming qualities, Landon. Now, would you please get out of my room?"

"After him," I said.

The guy looked to Andi.

She gave him a tired shrug. "I need to shower and get ready, anyway. We can catch up later. And thank you for last night."

"Thank you for last night?" I asked. "What the hell does that mean?"

"What is your problem?" Andi hissed.

"You," I said simply. The truth of my statement hit me with ten times the force of her potential lover's punch. In a literal sense, it was obvious. She stood between me and the club. She was the only thing stopping me from doing what was smart and squashing the doubts my members had—from going to the lawyers and taking everything William had dangled between us.

I had hoped I could start putting her out of my head after our fight. I knew I didn't deserve her forgiveness, and I hadn't expected it. But she'd wriggled her way into my brain and set up camp. When I closed my eyes, it was her I saw. *That* was a problem. A big fucking one. It was the exact moment I'd decided not to get attached to anyone again. There was the pain of caring about something and having it taken away, or the duller, more tolerable pain of not caring in the first place. I'd chosen the later.

Except.

Andi put her hands on my shoulder and literally pushed me

toward the door. I let her move me but didn't let her close the door until the other guy left. My blood boiled when he had the nerve to reach in and give her a long hug before he did, though. I refused to move from the doorframe when he tried to slide past, forcing him to bump into my shoulder.

"Go," Andi said. "Home. Back to New York. To a ditch, I don't care really. Just go."

I reached for her cheek, but she pushed my arm away.

"No, Landon. You don't get to fix it with a kiss this time." She shook her head, eyebrows scrunching together. "Just go"

I let her push me out the door and watched as the door slammed in my face.

Fucking wonderful.

CRASHING THE WEDDING AND ALL OF THE PRE-GAME FESTIVITIES was surprisingly easy, at least from a logistical standpoint. There were enough guests that Dana had apparently decided to just let people come and go without any form of security. I'd been able to walk into the hotel without having to explain who I was or what I was doing, and I'd even found a hallway full of unclaimed rooms. Conveniently, there was even an agenda with dates and times of every event for the wedding waiting on my bed.

I was lurking in the outer edge of the rehearsal dinner while I sipped on a cocktail. All around, little pockets of friends were catching up and laughing. All I could do was scan the room obsessively for Andi, or the piece of shit I'd found in her room this morning. I'd settle for either of them, because it would at least let me know they weren't together at the moment.

I wasn't sure what I hoped to gain from being here. Closure? Forgiveness? Whatever it was, I doubted I was going to get it.

Yet I still wanted everything—including the things I absolutely knew I'd never have a chance to take again. I still wanted to watch her beg. I wanted to unravel her. To ruin her. *Destroy every silky inch* of her.

The grin I'd been wearing melted when I saw her walk in with the guy from this morning. They were dressed to impress— her in some pretty little dress that couldn't hide the gorgeous body she had underneath, and him in a navy suit with a crisp white undershirt.

I straightened my tie and headed for them, shouldering past anyone who stood in my way.

Someone small got between me and them and I nearly ran them over. I was about to push her out of the way when I recognized her. "Bree?" I asked.

"Landon," she said slowly. "You know, you look like you're about to kill someone."

"One or two someones, maybe," I said, not looking away from Andi.

Bree followed my eyes and nodding knowingly. "Jealousy sucks. One time, I think I was like fourteen? I was dating my first real boyfriend and he was kind of a manwhore. So I just kept getting more and more jealous, like I thought I could stop him from being a slut by ordering him not to talk to anyone. Within a few weeks, I was literally having this conversation with him about why I didn't think he needed friends if he had me. *Yeah.* Just saying, jealousy is a dangerous, slippery road."

"I'm not fourteen. I'm also not jealous. I'm—" I took a long, deep breath. *I'm being an idiot,* is what I would've said if I was honest. *I fucked up so badly that I don't know what to do anymore, so I just showed up like a lost puppy hoping for one last morsel of attention it knows it doesn't deserve.*

Her eyebrows shot up. "You know," she said softly. "She told us everything."

I nodded.

"And she'd be an idiot to forgive you. Or trust you. Or even *like* you, after something like that."

I nodded again.

"But you're here."

Just past Bree, I could see Andi laughing about something with the other guy.

Andi's sister put a soft hand on my shoulder and gently led me to the side of the room. She looked up at me like *she* was the older and wiser one who was about to give me some much-needed advice. "Look. I've been rooting for you in this thing. But there is kind of a spectrum of screw ups. There's, 'oops, I left dinner in the oven too long and now we have to get takeout,' on one end. On the other end, there's, 'by the way, your adoptive grandfather is actually my dad.'"

"I get it. I fucked up. Royally. And I'm supposed to give up because of it?" I shook my head, teeth clenched. "I can't do that."

"No. But when you screw up as much as you did, it takes more than just bull-headedly forcing yourself back into her life. Take a few seconds to breathe. Think about what you did. Ask yourself what you'd need to do to earn her forgiveness. Because I'm pretty sure acting like a jealous asshole isn't going to cut it."

I sighed. Bree was right. I hated to admit it, but she was. I'd been watching Andi and Tommy the whole time she was talking. I thought I'd do my best to be good to Andi if she gave me another chance. I'd take care of her and appreciate her. But I'd thought the same of women I'd dated in the past. Maybe the level of intensity had been entirely different, but I'd never entered into a relationship thinking I'd wind up growing cold and pushing them away.

What was to say I wouldn't do the same to Andi? And now I'd be pulling her away from a guy who would probably treat her right—a guy who probably wasn't so internally fucked up that he couldn't stop himself from ruining good things when they came along.

"Is that your thinking face?" Bree asked. "Because you're just kind of glaring off into the distance and I can't tell if you're still planning to murder Tommy."

"You're right," I said. I reached down and ruffled her hair before leaving.

I had to remind myself a dozen times to not turn around and step between Andi and Tommy.

I needed to get out of there, and I needed to do it before I could change my mind. I knew what I had to do to start making this right. God knew if it'd be enough, but whether Andi forgave me or not, I wanted to be able to live with myself.

23

ANDI

I had to admit I was surprised when Landon never showed his face again. The wedding had been yesterday, and I'd never quite shaken the sense that he was going to confidently appear at any moment and melt Tommy with a glare. I think the idea that Landon would swoop in and destroy everything had inadvertently turned into a safety net for me. I let things with Tommy keep going, simply because I kept assuming Landon would show up to end it.

I'd spent the night talking and laughing with Tommy. He had let me listen to some of his drumming, and we'd even created our first inside joke after a waiter tried to take my drink away because he thought I was underage. At the end of the night, he'd walked me back to my room and I knew he was waiting to know if I was going to let him come in or not. And when he'd leaned in for what could've been a kiss goodnight, I hugged him instead.

Tommy thanked me for a wonderful evening, smiled, and said he'd see me soon.

It was all shaping up to be so insanely simple. Like the kind of thing I'd been waiting around my whole life to happen. Boy comes into my life. Boy is nice. Boy and I get along. Next comes marriage and a baby carriage. Except there was a dark undercurrent to the fairy tale.

Before boy met girl, girl met Landon. And Landon planted a poisonous seed of hunger in girl—a seed that girl was apparently too stupid or weak to flush out of her system. No matter how much girl should've wanted to let this thing with boy happen, she couldn't stop thinking about the dark prince who had tried to break her heart before she even gave it to him.

I was standing in front of the bathroom mirror in my room, and I let out a bitter laugh. I was on a dream trip where I'd just been able to attend a beautiful wedding in an amazing venue. My room was spectacular, and a really nice guy had practically fallen into my lap. All of that, and none of it had been enough to get Landon off my mind.

There was a knock at my door.

I took a look at myself in the mirror. I tucked a loose lock of hair behind my ear and then checked my teeth. I hurried to the door, took a deep breath, and pulled it open.

"Hey," Bree said. "Jeez. Don't try to hide the fact that you're disappointed to see me or anything."

I laughed. "Sorry. I'm not. I was just—" I shook my head. *I was just hoping you were Landon. That you'd come because you couldn't bear the thought of me being with someone else. That maybe you'd rumble something possessive about how I was supposed to be yours and you wouldn't stand for somebody else touching what belonged to you.* "What's up?" I asked as perkily as I could.

Bree leaned forward, making no secret of the fact that she was scanning my room for any extra guests. "Hmm..."

I put my hands on my hips. "It's just me in here."

"I see that."

"Did you need something, or were you just being nosy?"

"Just being nosy!" Bree said cheerfully. She gave me a soft little punch on the shoulder, a wink, and then strolled off. She even tried to whistle, but my little sister had never been a whistler. It sounded more like an elderly man breathing squeakily through his nose.

She was up to something. It was either something she'd already done, or something she was about to do, but Bree was meddling. For all the great things about my little sister, one of her faults was her tendency to think her perceptiveness about people was an obligation to intervene. In her mind, she felt like she could see the bigger puzzle—and when two pieces appeared to fit together, she couldn't help trying to make it happen.

I was packing my bags when Tommy stuck his head in the door. "Hey," he said.

"Hey."

"Catching your flight out today, right?"

"Yep," I said.

An uncomfortable silence passed between us, so I let my palms flap against my thighs and pressed my lips together in an approximation of a smile.

"Yeah, this is kind of weird," he said, echoing my thoughts. "I mean, I get it. We're out of town and everybody just was looking for ways to enjoy the weekend. But I'd still like to see you again. Maybe just to figure out if there's anything here."

"You live in Pennsylvania. It's a bit of a drive," I said. I wasn't even sure what I wanted at this point. Did I really want him to ask me about giving the long-distance thing a try? Did I want him to say he'd drive to New York every couple weekends to see me? Or was I trying to make excuses for him because I knew my heart was still foolishly stuck on the idea of Landon.

I didn't know.

All I knew was the way Landon still swirled in my thoughts like a shadow. Even now, I could practically feel the way he spread across the room, making everything darker by comparison. Would it really be fair to step into a relationship when another man had that kind of hold on me?

"I'm gonna be honest," Tommy said, laughing a little at

himself. "I really like you, Andi. You don't give a shit what people think. You're funny. And you're—" He gestured to me, clearly implying he liked the way I looked, too. "Point is, I'm willing to look a little pathetic and just ask, because I'll be kicking myself if I don't. Can I come see you sometime? I've got a cousin who lives in the Bronx, so I could stay with her and it wouldn't have to be weird. We could get coffee, I don't know. Just something?"

I smiled. It was a real smile, too. I was flattered, and it felt good to know a real guy—a normal, nice guy liked me enough to want to try to make this work. But I owed it to him to tell the truth. "There's something I should've told you from the start."

Tommy's expression fell a little, but he nodded. "That other guy, right? Tall, dark, and asshole?"

I grinned. "That one. I'm not dating him or anything, but... It's complicated, and it wouldn't really be fair to you if I didn't put that out there. Actually, he royally screwed up, and I was hoping I'd be able to put him behind me. But the truth is I'm still sort of hoping he'll find a way to make me forgive him."

"You have feelings for him?" Tommy asked.

"I don't want to, but... *yeah.* I think I do."

"I had an ex once. We dated three years before she cheated on me. But I still couldn't get over her. Not all the way. So I didn't date for like six months, and when I finally started dating again, it was a weight off my shoulders. I realized there were other people, you know? One can seem special, especially when you push everyone else away for them. But at the end of the day, there are more people out there. Nobody is worth holding your heart hostage."

I set the clothes down I was about to stuff into my bag and looked at him. "That actually makes a lot of sense."

He shrugged. "Personal experience, or something like that."

"You know what? Sure. We can get coffee and hang out sometime. I can't promise that..." I trailed off.

Tommy nodded. "Like I said. Been there. But I'm willing to give it a shot anyway."

I smiled. It might have just been the sun creeping out from the clouds outside, but I thought the Landon-shaped shadow hanging over the room faded just a little.

I spent the plane ride home trying to make less of a mess out of everything that happened. Mentally, I'd pull one string, thinking it could untie the whole muddled knot of emotions. *What if I just talk to him? Tell Landon it's over to his face? Maybe I'm having trouble letting go because I never really cut things off?* But it was no good. Nothing was going to end in a clear answer.

I was starting to wish I could just fold in on myself and disappear.

Hello melodramatic, it's me, Andi. I was beginning to get well acquainted with emotional angst, and if it got any worse, the next logical step was carrying around a little composition book dotted with skulls where I wrote angry poems about love.

Dear Landon
Roses are red,
Violets are blue,
Onions stink,
But so do you.

The problem was that I also couldn't stop wanting to put onions on everything I ate, even when cutting them made me cry and smelling them made me nauseous. Oh, and I was still inexplicably sexually attracted to those onions, no matter how mad they made me.

24

LANDON

It didn't take much digging to find out when Andi's flight would return. It also wasn't too hard to make sure I was in the hotel lobby during the rough window of time I expected she'd be coming back from the airport.

I knew it wasn't the time to talk to her—after all, I still needed to make a call before I had that conversation with her. I waited in the corner of the lobby and watched as she came in about an hour later. I'd never felt relief like I felt when I saw she was alone. No Tommy. No phone glued to her ear as she chatted up her new boyfriend.

It wasn't a guarantee that they hadn't decided to take things a step further, but it at least let me hold onto hope that she'd left whatever they had back in Florida.

Once she'd headed up in the elevators, I pulled out my phone. With a muttered curse, I put it back in my pocket and headed outside for my car.

I found my mom where she usually was. I could hear her coughing before I even got up the stairs to our apartment. Inside, she was on the couch with a show playing on the TV.

I clicked the show off, then sat beside her.

"I know that look," she said. She set down a cup of the tea she was always drinking and wrinkled her forehead at me. It was a look I'd seen dozens of times as a kid—when I'd come to her for advice or when she knew she'd have to explain something difficult to me.

"I'm going to give the club and the hotel to Andi."

I braced myself for the look of disappointment. I knew my mom was too good a person to show it openly, but I expected a flicker of something to pass over her features. I stared hard but didn't see anything.

"Okay," she said calmly.

"Okay?" I asked, my voice raising slightly in anger. "It's okay that I'm going to risk my mom's life? That I'm handing over our best shot at getting the money to get you the proper treatment? And for what?" I asked. I'd stood up at some point, hands clenched at my side. I closed my eyes and let out a long breath, sitting back down.

"Love?" she asked. "For doing what you think is right?"

I shook my head. "One sided love, if that's what it is." I looked up and pointed at her, eyes narrowed when I saw the way she was smiling. "And I'm not saying it *is* love. Hell, I don't even know how I'd know if it was."

She gave a little shrug. "You'd know. And seeing you so ready to give up the club you've poured your heart into? I'd say that's a decent sign, too."

"Mom," I said, almost pleadingly. "I need you to talk me out of this. Tell me you'll fucking hate me for risking your health over a girl."

"The only thing I'll tell you is to watch your damn language." She leaned back, then smiled after a brief pause. "If you told me you were going to rob someone to get the money to pay for my treatment, I wouldn't want it, anyway. If your gut is telling you this girl deserves her inheritance, then you give it to her. I don't care what my situation is. I only want your help if you can give it with a free conscience."

I lowered my eyes, nodding to myself. I'd partly come to tell my mom, but I'd be lying if I hadn't hoped she'd talk me out of it. If nothing else, that she'd tell me I was being an idiot.

I thanked her, gave her a hug, and headed back outside. This time, when I pulled out my phone, I made the call.

THE NEXT DAY, I WENT LOOKING FOR ANDI. I DIDN'T HAVE TO LOOK for long, because I was only two steps into the lobby of The Wainwright when I heard a familiar voice.

Grant was laughing about something. I looked toward the sound and saw him standing beside Andi with his hand on the back of her chair. He was smiling and so was she.

I had my limits, and Grant talking to Andi was way beyond them. All the man did was seduce women. It was like his cock had him at constant gunpoint to provide a never-ending supply of pussy. And now he was talking to Andi.

My Andi.

It took considerable effort not to run or throw something. Instead, I walked slowly and deliberately toward the two of them.

"Grant," I said.

He turned, saw me, and flashed a kind of terrified but crazy smile. "Oh, hey."

"So, you're still alive?" Andi asked. "I didn't realize Tommy hit you so hard in Florida. I guess you had to fly back here to see a specialist, or something?"

Grant's eyes bulged and he covered his mouth. He choked back a laugh, then straightened his face just long enough to speak. "Somebody hit you?" He laughed as soon as he finished speaking.

"You sound surprised," I said as calmly as I could.

"I don't know why, but the idea of someone punching you

really tickles me in the right places," Grant said. "You're always so serious." He turned to Andi. "What did Landon do after he got hit? Just kind of grunt and glare?"

"Grant," I said again. "I need to have a word with you. In private."

He raised his eyebrows, then smirked at Andi. "Didn't I say he'd say that?"

She nodded. "Word for word."

I wanted to groan in frustration. So Grant wasn't making a move over here. He was meddling. "You," I said, jabbing my finger into Grant's chest. "Go wait over by the bar. And you," I pointed at Andi. "Stay right there."

Grant gave me a quick salute, then wandered off while whistling a happy tune.

Andi, on the other hand, was sticking her furry-socked foot in my face. I could now clearly see that her sock was one of those hideous toe socks with a little slot for each of her toes, which she was wiggling. "Do I look like I'm planning on going anywhere?"

I was surprised by how much I wanted to take her by the hand and drag her down to the club. I'd only had the briefest taste of her submission, and even that had come with a caveat. She'd never fully bought in to the experience. All I had was one of those ridiculous, fuzzy sock-clad toes of hers dipped into the waters. I still wanted more, even if I knew it wasn't likely to ever happen.

She was watching me with the defiance in her eyes I'd come to crave. Her silky, almond hair was perfectly unkempt, and I didn't even think she was wearing makeup. Her raw beauty was making it impossible to focus.

"What did he say?" I asked.

"That you had been smiling like a little boy who just found his first porno mag when you met me, but now you're even broodier than usual since you screwed things up with me."

I might've smiled. Instead, I just felt an overwhelming urge to punch Grant in the dick.

I turned to shoot him a poisonous look. He was standing on the opposite end of the lobby but smiled cheesily and waved when he saw me looking.

"And you believe him?"

"You *did* fly to Florida just to check on me. A normal person would've tried a phone first."

"I texted you," I said. "And I didn't just go for you. I had business to take care of there."

"You basically growled at me via text one time. That doesn't really count."

"I didn't growl," I said tightly. "I asked where you were."

"*Where are you*," Andi said in a mockingly deep, scratchy voice. "Also, Grant told me you'd try to claim you were there on business. But he told me that you came because of me. *Curious*," she said, stroking her chin.

The whole time we'd been talking, there was a faint air of amusement in Andi's voice. Except I could feel that it wasn't the same light, carefree kind of way we'd talked before she knew the truth. She was reserving part of herself.

"What happened with Tommy?" I asked. I wanted to kick myself in the shin for being such an idiot. I'd told myself a hundred times not to ask. There were ways she could've answered the question I absolutely wasn't prepared to hear.

"It's not your business," she said. Finally, the humor in her voice was all gone. I could see the coldness and anger in her eyes now, staring right back at me.

"No," I said. "You're right. But there's something I need to tell you."

"Another secret?" Andi asked. "Are you going to tell me you're also distantly related to my cousin, Gator, too?"

Despite the gravity of the moment, I felt my lips threatening to spread into a smile. "*Gator?*" I asked finally.

"Yeah," Andi said. She looked up, then bit her lip slightly. It was a relief to see that she could at least forget to hate me in small spurts. "He's from Alabama. When Grandpa Willy died, he actually said if I needed a lap to cry on, I could come up to the cabin and if we needed some time alone, he could take the batteries out of 'momma's' scooter. Apparently, she might shout and make a fuss, but she wouldn't be able to get us."

I winced. "Isn't the expression a shoulder to cry on?"

"Unless you're hoping for a little incestuous bonding session," Andi said.

"Well, no," I said. "I'm not related to... *Gator*. I came to give you this." I held out the USB stick the lawyers had given me when I transferred the hotel and club to Andi.

"What is it?" she asked.

"Another video from William."

"Why now?"

I smiled tightly. "Don't know. This came from the lawyers. I haven't watched it."

She squinted down at it. "Both our names are on it."

"I should go," I said.

Andi looked like she was about to argue, but then her features hardened. She let me leave.

I took one last look over my shoulder because if everything played out the way I imagined; it'd be the last time I saw her.

MOM AND I WERE WATCHING A TV SHOW TOGETHER WHEN A KNOCK came at the door. It was getting late, and it was strange to think I didn't need to worry about getting to the club in time for it to open.

"Expecting someone?" asked my mom.

"It's probably Grant. Maybe James," I said, standing to get the door. I hadn't told either of them what I'd done, and I wouldn't have been shocked if they had found out by now.

I opened the door and saw all five foot nothing of Andi standing in the doorway. She was wrapped up in a scarf and coat against the cold and her nose was red.

"Andi..."

"Can I come in?"

I swallowed. I had never told her that James and I shared an apartment with my mom. I also hadn't told her about the cancer my mom was fighting. I knew how it would look if I let her in now. It'd practically demand her pity. So I slid out into the hallway and shut the door behind me, hoping my mom wouldn't have a coughing spell for however long it took me to handle this.

"What's wrong?" I asked.

Andi shot a curious look at my door, and then she seemed to think of something that made her angry. She held up the USB stick. "I decided you deserved to see this, too. Even if you are an asshole."

"You haven't watched it? And how did you know where to find me in the first place?"

"Grant told me. And no. I haven't watched it, so can I come in? Or are you going to hide something else from me just to round out your profile as the least trustworthy guy on the face of the planet?"

I swallowed. "It just wouldn't be a great idea for you to come inside right now."

"There's a woman in your apartment. Isn't there?" she laughed at herself without an ounce of humor in the sound. "I'm such an idiot. You've given me every reason to hate you and to never trust you again, and here I am still trying to—I don't even know what I was trying to do. But obviously I was stupid for trying, wasn't I? Because you've got—"

"Andi," I said, meeting her eyes. "My mom is very sick. My brother and I live with her to save money. I didn't want you to see that and think... I don't know. I didn't want you to think you were obligated to forgive me because of it."

Her eyebrows drew together. "What kind of sick?" she asked softly.

"Lung cancer. It's her third time. We just found out a few weeks ago and haven't officially started treatments yet."

She looked down, plucking idly at the USB with her fingers. "Now I feel like an asshole. I'm sorry, Landon. I shouldn't—"

"No," I said. "You're not in the wrong because I kept something from you. And you don't owe me anything. Okay? I don't want to win you back because you pity me."

"Win me back?" she asked. "Is that what you were trying to do?"

I blew out a long breath, then fixed my eyes on her. "No more half-truths. No more lies. Yes. I went to Florida to try to find a way to convince you to forgive me because I realized I'd regret it for the rest of my life if I didn't. Then I saw you with that guy. Once I was done wanting to rip his head off, I realized you were better off. It felt like swallowing acid to admit it, but I left because I also wouldn't have been able to forgive myself if I fucked up something good for you because I was too selfish to walk away."

"And what is this?" she asked, holding up the USB stick. "I think you know exactly why the lawyers gave it to us now."

I sighed. "Come inside. I have a feeling watching the video will explain everything better than I can."

25

ANDI

I followed Landon into the small apartment. He had admitted he needed the money from the club, but he hadn't been clear about why. He had also told me his mom was sick at one point, but I had stupidly assumed it was past tense. The new information was forcing me to see everything that happened from a new perspective.

The apartment was clean and smelled fresh, but it was clearly not the home of people with abundant amounts of money. Hearing Landon admit he wasn't really wealthy was one thing. Seeing it was another.

I smiled when his mom noticed me. She was pretty with Landon's dark hair and eyes, but the similarities stopped there. She sat up straighter and flashed a kind smile. "You must be Andi. I'm Loraine."

I nodded. "This is probably a little weird," I said. After all, my "grandfather" was her ex-husband. My sisters and I were the people he had apparently replaced Landon, his brother, and his mother with. I realized I wouldn't even blame them for hating us. How could they not?

"No. It's good to see you. To meet you, finally. Landon has already talked so much about you."

I shot a half smile at Landon, who was making himself busy in the cramped kitchen as he got tea ready. *Tea?* He didn't strike me as a tea drinking kind of guy, so maybe it was for his mom.

"I can go back to my room and give you two some privacy," Loraine said, starting to stand.

"You don't have to," I said.

"Don't worry, sweetheart. I'm either going to take a nap right here on the couch or in my bed. I'd prefer the bed."

Once she left, Landon stopped messing with the kettle and slowly walked back toward the couch, where I now sat. "Well, you really want to do this?"

I reached up to hand him the USB stick. "I do."

He pulled out a laptop and set it on the coffee table in front of the couch, plugged in the USB, and then opened the video.

Once again, we saw my grandpa sitting at his desk. It looked like it could've been filmed the same day as the video I'd first seen in the theater of The Golden Pecker, but I couldn't be sure.

"Well, well, well," Grandpa said. "You know, I always loved mystery books and thrillers. There was something about the grand flourish at the end that always scratched a deep itch for me. When I realized I had a chance to leave behind a few flourishes of my own, how could I resist?"

He paused, grabbed a bag of Skittles that was already open beside him on the desk, and popped a couple in his mouth. He chewed, showing no sign of being in a hurry to resume his little speech.

"So! Unless the lawyers fucked up and gave you the wrong USB, the fact that you're watching this means that things have played out in a very interesting way. I assume you both know by now that Landon tried to give the club *and* the hotel to Andi. And—"

I lunged forward, tapping the spacebar to pause the video.

"Wait. They must have given us the wrong USB. He just said you gave me the club and the hotel."

"Yeah," Landon said. "This is the right USB."

I blinked. "You wouldn't do that, though. You said it yourself. Your mom is sick, and you don't have the money to start your own club. Why would you just give everything to me?"

Landon didn't answer right away. When he did speak, his voice was quiet. "I was angry for a long time, Andi. Angry that my dad was never that good at being a dad in the first place. Angry that he tried to pit us against our mom after the divorce. Angry that he took you and your sisters in and suddenly figured out how to be a decent human being. The club became some kind of symbol for me. Like if I could just take it over and do well, it'd somehow send a message to him. Maybe a final middle finger, or something.

"It's going to sound ridiculous," Landon continued. "But I actually was most angry when he died because I knew he'd robbed me of the chance to prove I didn't need him. I wish it hadn't taken me so long to realize none of that really mattered. So I don't want it anymore. Any of it. I've got the education to get another job—one that'll help me start to pay for mom's treatments. I'll be fine."

It still felt like he was going to tell me this was all a bad joke any moment, but little by little, the truth was sinking in. The club and the hotel were mine, now. A minute ago, I'd been in financial trouble and on the verge of having to move out of the city entirely if I lost my room at the hotel. Now I was the owner of millions in real estate and a club that appeared to generate vast amounts of money every month.

It should've felt like a victory, especially after the way Landon had betrayed my trust. I was about to speak, but Landon unpaused the video and Grandpa Willy's voice cut across the silence.

"I know you were probably wondering how in the hell I

could've possibly been irresponsible enough to put your fate in Landon's hands, Andi. But there was actually a second secret set of stipulations that only my lawyers knew about. This part is probably going to make both of you a little mad, but..." Grandpa stuck his tongue out and waggled his hands by his ears. "I'm dead, so tough shit. It never actually mattered if you did the items on the list. All that mattered was what Landon tried to claim from the lawyers. If he tried to take all of your inheritance, he would've got nothing. The club would've stayed in limbo and potentially gone to James or Grant, but I never intended for you to run the club, Andi. Putting you through a little sexual deviancy is one level of screwed up but asking you to take over the management of a BDSM club would've been a step too far, even for me. If Landon tried to split it with you—to keep the club and give you the hotel, for example, he'd get what he wanted.

"But the fact that you're watching this video means neither of those things happened. And, to be honest, that's why I'm assuming you'll never watch this video. If Landon tried to leave you the hotel *and* the club, then I would have to admit I underestimated him."

Grandpa sighed, folded his hands, and looked directly into the camera. "Landon. I know I made a royal mess of things between us. By the time I was willing to admit that, our relationship was already so far gone that I knew there was never going to be any chance of repairing the damage. The best I could hope for was to help you find something meaningful to work towards. I thought that was what I gave you with the club, and it was why I never paid you more than I did. If I'd given you the easy money, I worried you would've never cared enough to strive for something.

"But I worried you started striving more to take over the club for the wrong reasons—to piss me off or send me some kind of message instead of for your own sake. And that's part of why I put you two together for this little list. I had a feeling Andi was exactly the right kind of stubborn to match your obstinance,

Landon. If you're watching this video, I can only assume I was right. You two are probably holding hands right now and smiling."

I turned my head to Landon, who was on the opposite end of the couch. I couldn't help grinning a little. *Not exactly, Grandpa.*

"Oh," Grandpa said. "I almost forgot. If Landon tries to leave you everything, he still gets the club. And he gets a personal apology from me. So, Landon. Congratulations. I may have screwed up with you at every possible turn, but somehow, you managed to come out of it all as a decent human being. And you bet your ass I chewed you out in the other videos, by the way. So consider being spared that your other reward.

"Well! That's pretty much it. Enjoy your new lives, you two. For me, it's back to being dead." He closed his eyes and tipped his head back, letting his mouth hang open dramatically. After a few seconds, he peeked, then gestured for someone to turn off the camera before the screen abruptly went black.

"Wow," I said slowly. "I need some time to think."

I got up from the couch and went for the door.

Landon started to stand, but sat back down, watching me with a solemn look on his face. "Will I see you again?"

I paused, hand on the doorknob. "I'm not sure."

26

LANDON

The club wasn't open for the night, but I'd come after watching William's video with Andi anyway. A few hours ago, I was resigned to the idea that it was gone from my life. All the years I spent trying to make it into what it is might as well have been dust.

I ran my fingers across the golden rooster emblem engraved into the center of the bar. It was mine. *Really mine.* But what had it cost me?

I laughed. Too much. It had cost me Andi. I hadn't really expected her to forgive me on the spot for giving her the club and the hotel, but part of me had hoped. At least I'd have all the money I could ever need to help mom get better. I knew I would've found a way regardless, but it was still a relief to take the mystery out of the equation.

James wandered into the lobby. He was wearing all black, like usual. "Going to share?" he asked.

I thought about telling him what William had told me in the video. In all likelihood, the lawyers probably had instructions to send a video to James or another one of the Wainwright sisters now that my little mission with Andi was complete. But for some reason, I didn't want to spoil William's plan, whatever it might be. If he did rope James in with one of the Wainwright girls, I wanted him to have a chance to work whatever magic he'd almost worked with me and Andi.

"Club's mine," I said simply.

James nodded, as if getting the club wasn't the sole purpose of my life for years. "What's your first move?"

"Clean out some of the members I should've removed a long time ago. Sydney and Edward would be a good start."

James hardly showed he had heard me. We both knew Sydney and Edward had connections, and not just within the clubs. Kicking them out could cause trouble for me down the line, but I didn't care anymore.

"What happened with the girl?"

"Take a wild guess."

"She wants to use your hollowed-out skull as a wine glass?"

I grinned. "Was that a joke?"

"No. That was a quote from one of your exes. The one you ghosted in the middle of your second date. *At my club.*"

I wasn't particularly proud of that memory. I didn't realize the girl had gone as far as wanting to drink out of my skull, though. "Anyway, yeah. I'm guessing Andi wouldn't mind having my skull as a trophy at this point."

"Actually," Andi said. "I prefer your skull inside your head."

I knew her voice the moment I heard it, but I still had to look to confirm it was really her. She was wearing her fuzzy unicorn sweater with the silly little golden horn jutting out of her chest again. She gave me a sideways smile and flicked the horn, making it flop back and forth a few times.

"I'd ask how you got in here," I said, lowering my gaze to the dildo in her hand. "But I think I am just going to make a mental note to work on securing the secret entrance."

She rushed forward and hugged me tight. I squeezed her back, then couldn't help laughing when something rubbery thudded into my neck. "Can you get your dick off my neck, please?" I asked.

Andi tossed the dildo to the side, where it landed, bounced, and nearly hit James in the foot. He stepped back, scowling down at it. He gave the both of us a look like we had lost our minds, then stalked out of the room, leaving us alone.

"You tried to give me everything," she said, her voice muffled by my shoulder. She pulled back and looked up at me. "The least I can give you is a second chance."

"I can promise you this," I said. "It'll be the last second chance you have to give me."

Andi squinted, then smiled as she tilted her head. "Well, yeah. Because if you screwed up again it'd be a third chance. Then a fourth..."

I grinned. "Okay. Then I promise you won't regret this."

She pursed her lips thoughtfully. "Oh, I probably will. But I think I'd regret it more if I didn't give you one last shot to woo me."

I laughed. "*Woo* you? Is that what Andi Wainwright is hoping will come of this second chance? I could go get some flowers. Maybe a little romantic music?"

"It's not my place to tell you how to win my heart, Mr. Collins. But I will say, I still haven't torn up your silly little contract. And, seeing as we're inside the club, I think that technically means I'm still your submissive."

The humor I'd felt swirling around in my chest took on a darker, warmer note. I stared, making sure I was following her correctly. She didn't look away, so I reached for her hand.

"But," she said, biting back a smile. "Maybe the contract only applies during regular business hours?"

I would've laughed at the way she was teasing me if I didn't want to drag her to a private room so badly it hurt. I knew I'd probably never feel like I deserved her forgiveness. That was something I'd need to come to terms with. But Andi was giving it to me anyway. The best I could do was to make sure she never regretted it. And *damn* did I plan to start in earnest as soon as I had an opportunity.

"So I'll see you in a few hours," Andi said, backing away without turning. "And don't worry." She flicked her unicorn horn again. "I've got an even sexier outfit set aside just for this occasion."

My mind filled with images of Andi in sheer dresses or skin-tight, revealing leather. Whatever she had planned, I wasn't sure I could wait a few hours for it. "I'll see you then," I said as calmly as I could.

"You hope," she teased, then she walked toward the exit. I was glad to see there was a little hop in her steps. The old Andi was back. The one who enjoyed trying to rile me up and test me.

"Hey," I called before she could get away. "Are you leaving this dildo for later, or did you want to take it for your next break-in attempt?"

Andi awkwardly shuffled back, picked up the dildo, and then tried to slap me on the cheek with it. I barely managed to dodge backwards.

She laughed, then looked suddenly troubled. "Good thing you dodged that. This bad boy is actually Audria's, and who knows where it has been."

As if she'd just told me to enjoy my weekend, she waved over her shoulder with the wobbly dildo and left.

Goddamn. I thought I might be in love with the woman. I just wished I knew if that meant I was losing my mind or not.

27

ANDI

Bree and Audria met me at a Japanese steakhouse a few blocks from the hotel. I'd promised dinner was on me, which, I supposed I could now afford about as often as I wanted. It was a strange feeling. Not as strange as the idea that I had a BDSM date with Landon tonight—but strange, nonetheless.

Bree and Audria sat with me at an otherwise empty table surrounding the hot cooktop.

"Miss big spender all of the sudden," Bree said with a suspicious note in her voice. "Either you robbed a bank, or this has something to do with the inheritance. Because I literally can't remember you ever offering to buy dinner for us."

I took that as my cue to fill them in on everything that had happened since the wedding. Bree had already figured out some bits and pieces, but Audria was clueless. By the time I was finished, both my sisters looked a little shaken.

"Wow," Audria said. "And you forgave him?"

"Why wouldn't she?" Bree asked. "What else can a guy do to say he's sorry?"

"I don't know," Audria said. She paused to thank our waitress, who set down bowls of hot clear soup and lettuce with ginger dressing. "Maybe something romantic, like a helicopter ride. A pilot writing, 'sorry I was such a piece of dick,' in the sky?"

"You mean a bunch of expensive stuff he couldn't afford?" Bree asked.

"Okay. I don't know," Audria said. "I just don't think I would've forgiven him. How are you supposed to ever trust him again?"

"I won't know unless I try," I said. "And think about how hard it must've been for him to get past hating me. I pretty much stood for everything that went wrong in his life. So it's a little more forgivable that he wasn't immediately looking out for my best interests."

Audria scoffed. "Whatever you have to tell yourself."

I felt unexpectedly annoyed. I had thought my sisters would simply accept the story and be happy for me. "You know? I hope someday you find a guy you actually fall for. Because maybe then you'll realize it's not as simple as just doing what makes logical sense. Yeah, logically, I should've probably kicked him to the curb. But I feel something when I'm with him—when I *think* about him. Like that's the whole reason we're all here in the first place. To feel something like that. It's like being alive, and everything after or before it was just this sort of gray, bland comparison."

Bree was smiling stupidly.

"What?" I snapped. "Are you going to join in and tell me I'm an idiot, too?"

"No," she said. "I was just thinking how that sounds an awful lot like love."

I rolled my eyes. "You're like five years old. What would you know about love?"

Bree pegged a crouton at the side of my head. It bounced off and landed back in her salad bowl. We all stared at it in mild confusion for a few seconds before bursting out laughing. Even Audria was laughing, although it was a mild—*don't worry, I'm still a stone cold bitch*—kind of laugh.

"Well," I said. "Whether you two agree or whatever you choose to call it, I'm happy. *Really* happy. And the happiness didn't come when I found out he'd left me everything or when I watched grandpa's second video. It came when I knew I was going to forgive him. So..." I lowered my head.

Audria sighed. "If he hurts you again, I'm going to make him regret it. Got that?"

I grinned. "Fair enough. But what if it's just a little hurt. Like if he uses one of his pervy little whips or paddles on me tonight?"

Bree made a ridiculous sound between a cat purring and a motorcycle revving up. "When did you turn into such a hoe?"

I laughed, but Audria was making a disgusted face.

"If he does that, then I'll scrap my thesis and change the topic to forcing the repression of memories. Because Andi's goofy ass getting spanked with a paddle isn't an image I want to live with."

I wiggled my eyebrows. "Don't worry. I'll try to snap a selfie for you if things get wild."

"I wonder if there are going to be videos for us soon," Bree said. "Not that I'm particularly in a rush, but it has been weeks now and we haven't even heard what grandpa left us in his will."

"Yeah," I said, thinking back to the contents of his second video, which I had decided not to fully explain to my sisters. I couldn't say why, exactly. Maybe I just couldn't help admitting how his insane plan for Landon and I had actually worked. If he had something similar in the works for my sisters, I didn't want to ruin it for them. "I have a feeling there's something coming for you guys. Soon."

28

LANDON

I knew Edward and Sydney wouldn't be likely to agree to meet me unless they thought they were about to get something they wanted, so I made sure my invitation was appropriately vague.

Sydney was the first to arrive. She was wearing something provocative, as usual. She smirked when I looked up, as if she'd caught me admiring her.

"I'm looking forward to this," she said. "My leading theory is that you're going to ask me to help you squash all these rumors in exchange for... *something*. I just can't figure out what it is you think you have that I'd want. Your body, maybe?" She made a show of looking me up and down. "Tempting. But I don't think that would do."

I really was going to enjoy this.

"I'll explain what's going on once he's here."

Edward arrived a moment later. His hair was slicked back, and he looked as pale and ominous as ever. He surveyed the room more cautiously than Sydney had, almost like he was expecting some sort of ambush.

"What is this, exactly?" Edward asked.

"No," I said. "I just wanted to tell you both personally."

Sydney set down the glass of liquor she was holding with a clank. That had earned her attention, it seemed.

"The club is mine," I said. "And my first act as the sole owner of The Golden Pecker is going to be stripping your memberships. Both of you are done."

Edward's face was dark. "You realize what this will look like, don't you? People will think you're outing me because you've got a problem with kinks you don't agree with."

"Anyone who thinks that is welcome to leave. Everyone else won't have trouble figuring out you're gone because you were an asshole who wanted to bend the rules."

Sydney was smiling cruelly. "Did you forget who my father is? Do you think he won't crush you for this?"

"This is my club now. If I have to rebuild it from the ground up, so be it. But I'm not going to let the fear of what might happen stop me from doing what needs to be done."

"Very noble," Edward said dryly. "I hope those principles of yours are going to pay the bills when this place is empty in a few months."

"Somehow," I said. "I think I'll manage. Put your coins on the bar and leave, or I'll call security, and have you dragged out. Actually, I'd prefer the second option much more if you wouldn't mind."

The clink of their coins hitting the bar was the kind of satisfaction money couldn't buy. They both left, and for all I knew, they were right. Cutting them out from the club might very well ruin me. It could cause a chain reaction of influential members leaving until I was left with nothing but my name on a piece of paper and an empty building. But just like trying to sign the club and hotel to Andi, it felt right.

For now, that was good enough.

29

ANDI

Landon met me at the secret entrance just after midnight.

He stopped, as if noticing my shirt for the first time. "Oh," he said quietly.

I grinned. I was wearing a black sweater with a little plush version of the alien from the movie *Alien* bursting out of my stomach.

"I'm not walking you through the lobby of my club with that thing on," he said. He was trying to sound serious, but I could tell he was trying not to laugh. "Take it off."

In what I could only describe as a wild combination of stubbornness, willfulness, and a dedication to be just downright being irritating, I pulled the sweater off and let it fall to the ground.

Of course, I also wasn't wearing a bra.

I wasn't exactly sure what I expected, but Landon practically lifted me off my feet in his hurry to kiss me. My legs instinctively wrapped around his waist.

It was everything I remembered.

Fire.

Energy.

His lips found mine in a hungry flurry of kisses. His palm found my breast and cupped. He ran his thumb across my nipple, drawing a gasp from me that he swallowed up with a kiss.

I broke off from the kiss, biting my lip. "As much as I don't want this to stop, I don't think... *this* in the hallway is going to help me finish the list."

Landon's eyes smoldered. "If you want me to take my hands off you, put those away."

"Is that a command, Mr. Dom?"

Landon looked like he was searching for the right words. Finally, he just laughed, shaking his head. "Teaching you to be a submissive is going to be more difficult than I imagined."

"What?" I asked. "Did I do something wrong?"

"No," Landon said after a short pause. "I actually prefer you exactly the way you are."

"Topless?" I asked.

He grinned. "Yes. But that's not exactly what I was talking about."

Once I had put my sweater back on, I followed behind Landon after a brief refresher course on the rules of submission. Eyes down. No looking at other men. No talking unless spoken to. *Yada yada.*

I more or less played by the rules as we made our way through the lobby. I did peek around, just taking in the sights as we headed for the tangle of hallways that led away from the room. As usual, music thumped loudly, handsome men led scantily dressed women from place to place, and others lounged at the bar. I still felt far from comfortable inside The Golden Pecker, but more and more, I was coming to appreciate it.

I'd always enjoyed books as a kid where the characters found some secret passageway in a closet or a basement that led them to another world. In its own, leather-clad way, the club was like one of those doorways. Nothing down here felt quite real—like the world was being held at bay by a thin barrier.

It helped me to see what Landon meant when I'd said I felt dirty in the sensory deprivation tub. He'd told me society couldn't reach me down here, and that I didn't need to feel guilty for enjoying myself.

I could see that's what this place was for the members. They were all probably businessmen and women, influential figures, and they probably all lived very normal, professional lives. But down here, they could let go. They could indulge without fear of being judged.

I'd been so hung up on the idea that I *should* be mad at Landon after he told me who he really was. Being here reminded me how easy it was to stop worrying about what I should do or what others might think. I could just do what I wanted.

And right now? Right now, I wanted to enjoy tonight. I wanted to give this whole crazy, wild, submissive thing a shot. And I wanted to hand the reins to Landon Collins.

He glanced over his shoulder at me and caught me looking around. Landon stopped, touched my nose softly, and lowered my eyes. I stole one last mischievous look at him and caught him grinning.

"I'm going to enjoy punishing you for that," he said in a low, growly voice.

I thought about what he might mean by that while we made our way deeper into the club. Eventually, we reached a door where Landon slid his coin in a receptacle like we'd seen outside the sensory deprivation room. It clinked in and the lock disengaged. Landon led me inside what appeared to be a bedroom.

For once, I decided to play nice and kept quiet, even though a dozen questions were swirling around my mind.

Landon closed the door, locked it, and then started walking a slow circle around me.

"Not completely submissive, but getting there," he said in an almost appraising kind of voice. "So there's at least potential that you can be trained."

I looked up.

He clicked his tongue, but the grin he wore was wicked. "The good news for you is I'll enjoy training you."

"What now?" I asked quietly. I would've continued trying to play my role, but it felt like he was waiting for something.

"Now," he said, "I give you one last reminder because you're still new to all of this. Yellow means we're nearing your limits. Red means stop, no questions asked. Understand?"

I nodded. There was a slight difference between the Landon I had come to know and the Landon I saw when he was playing the role of my dom. His voice was sharper. Things that might've seemed like suggestions carried the weight of command. I thought I understood what he was doing, because I also had to change slightly to even try to fill the shoes of a submissive. The normal me was so far from submissive that it was almost laughable. Landon might not have had to stretch as much to be dom-like, but in some way, it helped me better understand it.

"Can I ask a question?" I said.

Landon seemed like he was actually considering saying no, but then he nodded.

"Hypothetically. Let's say you and I wound up... *together*. What would happen if I decided I didn't want to keep doing all of this?"

"Then I guess it would be the end for us," Landon said.

I stared.

He flashed the shadow of a smile. "To tell the truth, I hadn't thought about it. BDSM has been part of my life for a long time now. Being here. This club. I guess it was a way of trying to grab control in my life. For as long as I could remember, everything was always just changing so fast and nothing I ever did could stop it. Here, though? I thought if I could just take over the club one day, I'd finally have the control I wanted. But I care more about you than any of that. I'd still give up the club for you if that was what it took, Andi."

He put his hand on my cheek, eyes falling to my lips and then lifting back to meet my gaze. "Because I love you."

My throat felt dry, and it might have had something to do with the fact that you couldn't properly hydrate yourself on a liquid intake of Diet Coke, candy, and a few pounds of rice and chicken. But I also hadn't expected *that.*

I tried to remember how long I'd actually known Landon. Was it insane to be dropping "L" bombs after... what, a few weeks? Especially only hours after I'd finally forgiven him for lying to me? But there it was again. I was thinking about what someone else would think or say if I told him I loved him too. I hadn't even stopped to ask myself what I felt.

"I love you too," I said. "But," I stick a finger in his face, "you can still screw this up, so don't get too excited. And I'm willing to give all of this a shot, by the way. I was just curious."

Landon gently took my finger and lowered it. "A good submissive doesn't jab fingers at her dom."

"Unless it's up his butt?" I asked sweetly.

Landon was trying not to laugh, but he failed. "No. If you want to keep your job as my submissive, you will definitely not be putting your fingers up my ass."

I wiggled my eyebrows. "Some things are worth losing jobs over. Like talking back to a rude customer. Standing up for your principles against your boss. *Piercing your dom's dark star...*"

Landon laughed louder now, then cringed, as if he was picturing it. He took a deep breath, smoothing his features. "Okay. You make this much more difficult than it should be. Where was I?"

I pointed to the spot on the floor he'd been standing for the past few minutes. "Right there, dom, sir. You haven't really moved for a little while."

Landon glared. "No more games."

I looked down at the floor, doing my best impression of someone who doesn't have a few sarcastic responses floating around in their head.

30

LANDON

It took a hell of a lot more effort than it should have, but I eventually got my mind right. From the moment I'd met her, Andi had a way of making me feel like I was off-balance. That might have made some men uncomfortable. For me, it was refreshing.

"This room is mostly normal," I said. "There are a few little bells and whistles that might make things more enjoyable, but for all intents and purposes, it's just a bedroom. If you find this to your liking, there are all sorts of devious paths we can take in the future. For now, I have a feeling this will do just fine. *Now...* Take off everything but your panties and lay on the bed. Face down."

Andi shot me a nervous look. I was impressed when just a few seconds later, she peeled off her hideous sweater again and let it fall. It took almost all of my willpower not to go to her at that moment and pull one of her beautiful, hard nipples into my mouth. Instead, I stood and waited.

She paused, took a deep breath, and then unbuttoned her jeans. They were so tight she had to wiggle her hips to shimmy out of them. I let out a low, quiet groan I hoped she didn't hear as

I watched. Her skin was absolutely milky and flawless. The little pink thong she wore gave me a tantalizing view of the bikini-shape of her tan lines.

Andi did a little hop as she yanked on her jeans to get her foot out, and then lost her balance. In a confusing second, she had fallen to the ground with a thump. She let out a sound like a deflating balloon, then rolled over and covered her eyes. Her jeans were still tangled around one of her ankles.

I had to press my hand to my mouth to stop from laughing. It didn't seem like she'd actually hurt anything, but I thought I should be sure. "Are you okay?"

"That depends," she said, voice heavily muffled by the carpet she was talking into. "Can a bruised ego get infected?"

"I'm going to help you with these, since it seems too dangerous for you to do alone." I eased the jeans off her ankles, not missing the opportunity to appreciate my view. Her ass was only inches away, and my eyes followed the fabric of her thong to the slight mound of her pussy. I bit my lip hard, fighting back the urge to reach out for her.

"Do I stay here, or do I get up and try again? You never covered what happens if a submissive fails to perform a task."

I grinned to myself. "Because I have never heard of a submissive failing to walk across the room without injuring herself."

"Funny," Andi said.

I helped her to her feet. "Try again."

She walked to the bed, then jumped and spread her arms, landing on the soft comforter with a dramatic *woosh*.

Apparently, I was going to need to get more specific with my commands when it came to Andi. *Take off your clothes. Carefully. Walk to the bed and get on it like a normal human being and not like a five-year-old getting into the pool.*

I knelt beside the bed and opened a drawer in the frame. Inside, there were soft-tipped whips, flails, riding crops, paddles, and all sorts of bondage equipment plus an assortment of vibrators and insertables. Most of it was far, *far* more intense than anything I personally preferred to partake in. I grabbed a stiff leather riding crop. In the wrong hands, it would've been a brutal tool that could do serious damage. The way I intended to use it was going to be exceedingly gentle.

"What you feel," I said, lowering the tip of the crop—a thin, folded over strip of leather—to the small of her back, "is a riding crop. I thought it was appropriate, given that you're going to be about as easy to break in as a wild horse."

Andi rolled her head to the side so she could see me with one eye. "Did you just compare me to a horse?"

"Only your temperament," I said. I gave a light little whack on her ass with the crop. It was roughly the same force you'd get from bringing two fingers down on the back of someone's hand. Enough to startle, but not even sting.

She jumped, which I knew was mostly from the surprise. Still, part of what I needed to do was assess her pain tolerance, among other things.

"Did that hurt?" I asked. I ran the tip of the crop back up her spine while I waited for a response.

"No. Not really," she said.

"Good. That was a warning. You're my submissive, and I expect you to wait until I ask you to speak or give you permission to speak freely.

Her lips curled upward at the corner. "Yes, sir."

I knew she was trying to be surly, but the way *sir* sounded as it rolled off her tongue sent a warm rush through me. I continued moving the crop against her bare skin in a slow pattern. The way goosebumps sprouted up in its path was mesmerizing, making her soft skin look so touchable it almost hurt to keep control.

But this was part of what I enjoyed. Waiting to take what I wanted from Andi was only going to make the moment of indulgence that much sweeter. The longer I tormented her, the more I drove myself wild with need.

"Pain is a means to an end. A little injection of pain at the right moment is like a clean slate. Pleasure builds, and builds, and builds," I said, lowering the crop to her inner thighs and letting it brush her swollen lips. Then I flicked my wrist lightly, giving her another tap on the ass that briefly made her skin turn pink. "And the pain brings you right back to the start line. So that every touch is like the first again."

Andi was breathing heavier now. The movement of her chest was making her body rise slightly with each inhalation, so I could start to judge how she was reacting.

I needed to read her carefully—almost supernaturally. I needed to know where her line was and help her work her way to that point until a single, light breeze could push her over the edge. I brought the riding crop down again and dragged it in a slow circle between her legs, then used my hand to urge her legs open wider.

She gasped.

My cock was already painfully hard, but when I saw the fabric of her panties slowly darken with her arousal, I had to close my eyes it hurt so bad. I wanted to feel her pussy gripping every inch of my length—to bury myself in her as deeply as I could. I wanted everything she had and more, but still, I waited.

"I'm going to slide your panties down, now," I said calmly.

Andi's breathing hitched, but after a few seconds, she was breathing normally again, so I reached for the waistband and pulled them down. I drank in the sight of her, committing every curve and crevice to memory as best I could.

"Now roll onto your back," I said.

Andi obeyed. It was like in the sensory deprivation room. Her wall of jokes and sarcasm was far thicker and harder to penetrate than anyone I'd ever met, but there was a point where she could submit. She was there now, and *God*, it was the hottest fucking thing I'd ever seen. Knowing my wild, obstinate Andi was lurking just behind those docile, willing eyes was sexy as hell, even if I couldn't quite explain why.

I set the riding crop back in the drawer and pulled out a candle and a box of matches. "Now," I said. "This part is going to sting just a little."

31

ANDI

The match whispered against the box and hissed to life. It cast an orange glow on Landon's features, reminding me how many times I'd compared him to a devil.

I thought about how wrong that had been. He wasn't a devil. He was far from it. Landon was someone more like me than I'd imagined. The difference was I'd learned to protect my heart with a thick tangle of humor. Landon covered his in a false veil of darkness. Anyone who got too close would have their mouth filled with poison, just like I had. But I guess it took a combination of my willful grandfather and my own stupidly stubborn nature to get through it to the good guy beneath it all.

Landon moved the candle lower, drawing my attention. When he spoke, his voice was low and controlled—almost hypnotic. It felt like I was being led through some sort of ritual.

"Some areas of the body are more sensitive than others," he said, tilting the candle so a little droplet of hot wax fell just below my collarbone. I jolted against the sudden heat, but it passed as quickly as it had come.

I let out a breath, relaxing a little when I realized the pain wasn't anywhere near what I'd imagined.

"Others," he said, dripping wax just to the side of my nipple. "Are very sensitive."

I wiggled against the burn, which took a little longer to subside than the first had. It wasn't quite unpleasant, and I definitely wasn't into "yellow" territory yet, but it had gone from barely registering on the pain scale to something that was at least worthy of a little fear.

Suddenly, the idea that Landon had complete autonomy to drip his hot wax wherever he could reach on my body felt a little more sinister. Just as I was letting nothing turn into a slight bout of panic, he bent his neck and pressed his lips to the spot where the first drop of wax had landed. With his tongue, he detached it from my skin and then pulled it away with his teeth. He pulled the small circle of wax from between his teeth without breaking eye contact.

A shiver of pleasure throbbed in my lower belly.

Okay. If the game is that every bit of wax is going to get cleaned up by his mouth, then sign me up.

He dripped four more spots of wax from my sternum down to my hip next. The most painful was the one that landed near my belly button.

Landon bent again, sucking off the wax from my breast, my chest, and all the way down to my belly so that his face was nearly between my legs. A pleasant, warm hum was growing down there—like a familiar song working its way toward the crescendo. Except there was nothing familiar about this song, and I had no idea how far we were from the climax.

"Our brains do strange things when it comes to pleasure and pain," Landon said. He spoke in an almost distracted way, like a master explaining his craft while his hands were busy with the work. "While different, they are similar in surprising ways."

Another drop of wax.

I squirmed, fighting the urge to bat at it with my hands as the sense of scalding heat lasted two heartbeats, then three. This time, he didn't make me wait before using his mouth to sooth away the sting. He carefully kissed the spot. After the heat of the wax, his mouth felt deliciously good, like slipping into crystal springs on a hot day.

"But sometimes," he said. He set the candle down and started to strip off his tie, then his jacket, and then he worked his way down the buttons of his shirt. Each button revealed more and more of his well-muscled torso. "Sometimes all it takes is the memory of pain to intensify the pleasure."

I turned his sentence over in my head a few times, trying to puzzle out exactly what that meant was coming next. First, he'd slapped me around with his little leather stick. Not so bad. It had been more like getting hit with a feather because he had such a light touch with it. Then the wax had been a step more extreme, but I'd also thoroughly enjoyed the part where he removed it with his mouth.

So, what came next? Was he going to throw baseballs at me and then try to soothe away the sting with a vibrator? Or maybe his fingers?

"Why are you grinning?" he asked.

I cleared my face. "*No reason,*" I said meekly. *Maybe because I'm thinking stupid, silly thoughts? Or because it feels like if you so much as lay a finger on my clit, I'm going to explosively come?*

Landon considered me, then let his shirt fall to the ground. For all his iron and seriousness in here, I didn't fail to note the distinct bulge in his pants. It helped to remember that no matter how awkward I might feel laying here and being completely out of my element, he was still enjoying this.

I was waiting for him to dig something new out of his little bag of tricks below the bed, but instead, his hands went to his belt. My eyebrows climbed as I listened to the soft, tantalizing jingle of him pulling it free. His pants slid down just a fraction of an inch, giving me a glimpse of the sharp way his muscles cut diagonally down toward his cock. I wondered how much trouble

I'd be in if I reached out and touched it. The thought was tempting, but I also was far too curious to see what he'd do if I kept behaving, so I controlled my urges.

I heard him kick off his shoes, then he pulled off his socks and pants. He was only wearing a pair of black briefs that made the outline of his erection deliciously clear.

Watching him undress was fascinating, and not just because he was built like an underwear model with the face of a brooding movie star. He was so unabashedly confident. There wasn't an ounce of self-consciousness, even though he could clearly see me feasting with my eyes as he stripped for me.

He looked down at the drawer where he'd pulled the riding crop and candle from, then hesitated. His eyes flicked back up to me, almost as if a thought occurred to him—a thought he was trying to push down.

Landon kicked the drawer closed, then reached to pull me toward the edge of the bed and roll me on my side so I was facing him. "Suck my cock," he said. "And don't use your hands."

Oh. It was the first time I was glad I had a safe word. It wasn't that I wanted to say "no" in any capacity or that I was scared. Instead, it let me look at his commands and the possibility of what was to come in an entirely different way. It was exciting. There was no danger here. It was like a ride where I could slam the "stop" button if it got to be too frightening.

I noticed that Landon waited a couple seconds before he hooked his thumb in the elastic of his underwear and tugged it down. I assumed he was giving me a chance to use the safe word.

His dick sprung free, wobbling a little comically in front of my face.

I grinned up at him. "Penises are kind of funny. You have to admit," I said.

Landon glared down at me. He didn't look like he was particularly in the mood to talk about how goofy it was that men had these floppy appendages between their legs.

I was forced to take a deep breath, lick my lips, and stop trying to stall. I had actually never done this before, but I wasn't about to admit that to Landon. Then again, I'd eaten ice cream cones, bananas, and my fair share of lollipops, so how hard could it be?

I wiggled toward him slightly in a not entirely erotic way— given that I was on my side. For some reason, my first move was to plant a kiss right on the head of his cock. I had to hold back a goofy smile when it twitched in response. *Oh, you like that, do you, big guy?*

I opened my mouth and eased the first inch or two of him inside my mouth. I quickly realized I needed to open wider to avoid scraping him with my teeth. I snuck a look up at him and saw him looking down at me with a curious expression.

Shit. He was figuring me out, wasn't he? He knew this was my first time.

I decided to pull out the real moves. The only problem was I didn't have any real moves. So, I just tried my best to look like I knew what I was doing. I moved my head up and down, stealing glances up at him as I did.

When I remembered I had a tongue and started swirling it around or running it along his shaft as I moved, I felt the way his whole body tensed. His eyes were closed tight now, and his hands started threading through my hair.

Okay. I can see how this could be fun.

Soon, I felt like I was getting the hang of it. You might even go as far as to say I was a natural when it came to sucking dick. In any other context, I was fairly sure that would be an insult. In this case, I was happy to embrace my hidden talent.

Landon started to breathe heavier, and I felt the first real pulse of power.

I had all six feet plus of him and all his complex emotions and broodiness at my mercy. Each little flick of my tongue was practically a joystick I could use to drive him where I wanted. The feeling of having him at my mercy like this could get addicting, even if I was fairly sure it wasn't the takeaway I was supposed to get as his submissive.

My pace naturally increased as my own arousal got tied up in the act. At first, I'd been blindly trying to figure out what to do. Once I got the basics down and sensed his enjoyment, it became hot as hell for me, too.

I was tempted to put my hand between my legs to ease the growing need there, but I also didn't want to disobey. I was supposed to do what he told me, and right now, he'd told me to suck his cock.

"Fuck," he said, pulling back. I couldn't be sure, but I thought it was because he was about to come, except he wasn't ready to spend his pleasure yet.

I sat up, wiping the corner of my mouth with a finger. I saw him watching, so I decided to be a tease and I sucked my finger clean. Except, I realized, it was kind of counterproductive since it was my own saliva I'd just wiped from my finger, which I'd *cleaned* by coating it in more saliva. Either way, Landon seemed to enjoy it.

"I thought I wanted your submission all the way. But I don't want our first time to be tangled up with any of that. I want you. *Just you*," he said, stepping closer and cupping my face.

"You mean like I'm allowed to say stupid, sarcastic things again?"

He grinned faintly. "Whatever makes you happy."

"Then can I just say that you didn't extinguish that candle before you set it down, and I've been pretty nervous we're going to end up burning the place down. Also, you—"

He pressed a finger to my lips. "I'm not saying this as your dom. But I do think it's worth mentioning that it will be easier to fuck you if you're not talking."

I raised an eyebrow, then motioned like I was zipping my lips.

He got on the bed, advancing toward me so that I scooted back until my head was on the pillow.

"Green," I said.

"What?" he asked.

"Well, we had yellow and red. I figured I could just go on the whole traffic light theme and say 'green.' You know, like, let's do this thing. *Bow chicka bo*—"

Landon shut me up with a kiss, which I wasn't going to complain about.

I pulled back for a second. "Is it weird to kiss after I was, *you know?*"

"Can I change my mind about the whole submissive thing?" he asked.

I smirked. "Sorry. I just had to be quiet the whole time coming in here and it builds up."

Landon started kissing me again. As much as I wanted the whole experience, I thought I could've lived in this exact moment forever. His hard body was warm against mine, pumping slightly so that I could feel his length pressing between my legs, even if it wasn't inside yet. He was so *big* in every way. It felt like I could've survived a hurricane if I just held onto his broad back tightly enough—if I didn't break away from the kiss.

After a few minutes, he angled his hips so that I felt the head of his cock start to press against me. I was so wet that it only took a few gentle thrusts for it to slide inside.

I gasped, squeezing his back so hard I was afraid I might hurt him, but I couldn't manage to make myself let go.

Even though it wasn't really my first time, it felt like an entirely new experience. Every nerve in my body lit up when he was inside me. Maybe it was like he said—the little bursts of pain from the hot wax and the riding crop had somehow intensified the pleasure I felt now.

But I didn't think that was it. I thought it was more that I had gradually come to understand the pain Landon felt. I understood how his father had replaced him with my sisters and I—how he'd been left to handle the burden of his sick mother and how Grandpa Willy had tried to make him feel guilty for that. Most importantly, I understood how much he must really have cared for me to set all the anger aside and share a moment like this with me.

I squeezed my eyes shut and arched my back. I wrapped my legs around him, letting him drive himself even deeper inside me. A low, hungry moan spilled from my lips. I didn't know how badly I'd wanted to be filled by him until now, but *God*. It felt like heaven.

I didn't know how long it was before my body started to shake and an orgasm ripped through me. It felt like every drop of energy I had poured itself into the moment, making white lights flash in my eyes and rippling warmth run across my skin.

I almost didn't realize Landon had pulled himself out of me. He let his cock rest on my pelvis as it twitched several times, covering my belly in his warm come. I lifted my head to look. Landon's face was a mask of pleasure and his throbbing cock was still laying on my skin, glistening. I could hardly believe I'd just done that. With him. Here. That it had felt so good. I still hadn't even come completely to terms with the fact that I'd forgiven him.

All I knew was that I was so, *so,* incredibly happy it had led me to this moment.

"Would this be a bad time to tell you I'm allergic to sperm?" I asked.

Landon took a moment to register what I said, then he practically jumped off the bed and ducked down to look for something. I wondered how long I should let it go before telling him I was kidding and decided he *did* say I was off the hook as his submissive for tonight. Maybe he'd regret that by the time I was done.

He returned with tissues and some sort of hand sanitizer, which he started vigorously using to clean me off.

He stopped when he saw the grin on my face. "Wait," he said. "Did you make that up?"

"No comment."

Landon ended up in bed beside me. I was glad that he decided to stay completely naked. Under the silky covers and heavy comforter of the bed, I still couldn't get enough of the warmth of his bare skin against mine.

"Does this mean I'm your girlfriend now?"

Landon smirked. "Call it whatever you want. All I know is I'm not letting you go after that."

I gave him a thoughtful look. "Literally, or figuratively? Because I wasn't kidding at the aquarium when I said I have a small bladder. I'm currently waging war with my desire to not ever move from this spot and the need to go pee. *Also*, I've read that you're supposed to pee right after you do it. Less risk of a UTI."

Landon was watching me with a funny expression.

"What?" I asked.

"It's cute when you say *do it*, like you're some blushing virgin. Sometimes, you seem surprisingly crude. Then you remind me that there's this strangely shy, innocent side of you, too. I like it."

"Wait, blushing virgin. Are you saying I wasn't *good*?"

Landon frowned. "Hell, no. That was... It was enough that if you said you never wanted to even think about BDSM again, I wouldn't care."

I gave a little shrug. "I don't know. The whole candle thing was pretty hot. *Pun int—*"

Landon covered my mouth and rolled his eyes. "Although, I think a ball gag might come in handy from time to time."

"What's that? Like... You shove your balls in my mouth and gag me with them? That honestly sounds pretty much a hundred percent unpleasant."

"Uh, no. It's a little ball connected to straps. The ball goes in your mouth and the straps tighten around your head so you can't pull it out. It keeps you from talking."

I scowled. "You're saying my constant stream of nervous jokes are a turn off, Landon Collins? Because it's a package deal. You want access to the goods, then you've got to deal with the jokes."

"That's an arrangement I could live with."

I rolled on my side and planted a kiss on his lips. "Are there normal bathrooms in here? Because if you tell me I'm going to have to pee in a chamber pot, that will be the last straw."

32

LANDON

I sat in my small apartment staring at the first real check I'd ever earned from The Golden Pecker. With access to the accounts, I'd known roughly what I would earn as the sole owner of the club. Seeing it in my hands was an entirely different feeling.

Eighty-two thousand dollars and change from two weeks. Even with taxes and overhead taken out, I'd still be looking at roughly eighty thousand dollars of profit in two weeks. It was enough that I could put a deposit down and get mom to see one of the top specialists in the country this week. I could pay for in-home care if she preferred it and keep her away from as many lengthy hospital stays as possible.

My mom came shuffling out in a pair of fuzzy bunny slippers and saw me holding the check. I'd filled her in on mostly every-thing that had happened, including the fact that Andi and I were now considering ourselves a couple. That particular thought made me crack a bit of a smile. There was an odd sort of pride to having claimed Andi as a girlfriend—and the word *claim* was highly appropriate. She wasn't the sort of girl you fell into a relationship with. You had to wrestle her into submission, and even then, it wasn't a true kind of submission.

Andi wasn't for the taking. You never truly had her in your grasp. She was still wild, but she was *my* wild thing. I found that I deeply liked that about her.

My mom cocked her head when she saw me holding the check. "What's that?"

"First chunk of real money from the club," I said. "Looks like we might be flying out to California for that proton therapy thing you were talking about."

She raised an eyebrow. "What about Andi? You're not going to just leave her here in New York while you shuttle me around the country, are you?"

I waved the check. "With this, I can afford to get her tickets, too. I know she'll want to be there for you."

My mom scoffed. "Please. Following your sick mother around for her cancer treatments is hardly the way to celebrate a new relationship. Let me do this first treatment by myself. I'm still perfectly capable of getting around on my own. You two enjoy each other. When it's time for the next treatment, *then* I'll let you start doting all over me again. How does that sound?"

I scowled. "You want me to send you to California by yourself? No. Out of the question."

She pinched my cheek hard but smiled crookedly. "Just because you're bigger than me, it doesn't make you the boss, young man."

"This is really what you want?"

"Yes. Besides, I can drag your brother along if I decide I need the company. God knows he's not chasing any girls around."

I grinned. *No.* For some reason, the girls chased him. And he growled the majority of them away, too. Sometimes, I wondered what he was waiting for. I'd seen him date before, but he'd never really fallen for anyone.

I pushed my thoughts back to my mom. "Okay. Fine. But I'm

going to have someone waiting at the airport for you in California to make sure your ride is arranged, and your luggage is picked up. You'll be completely taken care of."

She blew off my words with a wave of her hand and a knowing smile. "I know you will, sweetie. Because you're a good boy."

It still amused me to hear her call me a boy. I knew I was far from it, but the way mothers never really stopped seeing their children as babies defied all reason and logic. To her, I was still the wounded little boy who had tried as hard as he could to hold her and my dad together. Ultimately, I'd failed at that. But somehow, finding Andi was the first thing I'd ever done that made me think I could start moving on from my past.

I paid Andi a visit at her friend, Rachel's, small apartment. I'd waited for her outside the place shortly after we met because Andi was trying to ghost me, but this was my first time coming up to the door. I knocked and waited.

Andi opened the door with a confused look on her face. "Is everything okay?"

"Yeah, absolutely fine," I said. "I just wanted to—" I caught a glimpse of the room. It was cluttered with stacks of papers, dirty clothes, and there was even a bra hanging on the radiator. There was even a disgusting, long rodent creeping around on the floor. I thought it might be a possum, but I also wasn't too sure I knew what they looked like. Andi's "boss," Rachel, didn't seem to notice or care that I was getting a glimpse of all of it. "Wow," I said.

"I know." Andi pushed past me and closed the door so we were talking in the hallway. "Rachel is kind of like a mad genius minus the genius part."

I grinned. "So she's just crazy?"

Andi thought for a second. "Yes, but no. She's... *driven*. But seriously," she said, punching my chest lightly. "Tell me why you're here or I'm going to start assuming the worst. Like you caught my gonorrhea or something."

I grinned. "Funny. But I was actually hoping to ask if you would accompany me tonight. To The Golden Pecker," I added in a lower tone.

She made a face. "As your submissive, you mean?"

"Yes," I said. Little by little, I'd been breaking her into my world. It was a slow process, but she seemed to be enjoying it. I knew I was.

"What about your mom? Didn't you say payday meant you were probably going to be out of town for a while handling her treatments?"

I shrugged. "Mom's orders. We're supposed to enjoy each other while she does this one on her own." I held up a finger when it looked like Andi was going to argue. "And yes, I know. I already tried talking her out of it, but she's insisting. I'll make sure she's fine, though."

Andi sighed, then toyed with my tie. "I guess if you *and* your mom want to twist my arm. We can do that. But I promised my sisters I'd take them to somewhere tonight. It's kind of a surprise, and I'm not telling you because I don't want you blabbing to them. So tomorrow, instead?"

Now it was my turn to sigh. I'd hardly been a day without her since we slept together. Every time I got a taste of her, it only seemed to make me want it more. She was dangerous, but I was loving every second of it. "Tomorrow, then. And this thing with your sisters. No men are involved, are they?"

"Hmm. Is that jealousy, I'm sensing? Do you really think any guy could compete with you, though? I mean, really. Who else am I going to find that can do that thing you did with the feather?"

I grinned. I had to admit I was a little proud of that particular trick. "You make a good point. And still no contact from Tommy, your little Florida fling?"

She smiled in a way that told me she secretly enjoyed my

possessive streak. "Yes, actually. And I told him to hop on the first plane available so he could—"

I growled a little playfully, backing her into the wall and looming over her. "Careful. Get me too jealous and I'll need to fuck the mischief out of you."

Andi batted her eyelashes up at me. "And what if your attentions only make me more mischievous?"

I grinned. "Then I'll enjoy the never-ending challenge that is taming you."

"My sister said I needed a guy who could tame me once," Andi said, almost thoughtfully. "Maybe I just needed a guy who was willing to accept he never could."

I chuckled. "I don't know about all of that. But I do know you're mine, no matter how much you might try to frustrate me."

"Try and succeed," Andi added.

"So, what did you really tell him. And I'll know if you're lying," I added.

"I told him that I fell in love with the devil, and that he should pray for my soul."

I laughed. "Did you really?"

She winked, then licked her lips. "Kiss me, and I might consider telling you the truth."

The door swung open just as our lips met. Rachel was glaring with her hands on her hips. "You know these walls are thinner than rice paper, right? I can hear everything. And I'm not paying you to be out here talking dirty to your—" Rachel seemed to look at me for the first time. Her eyes scanned me from head to toe, then she pursed her lips. "This guy is the Landon you've been talking about?"

Andi pointed a finger at her warningly. "Don't say anything weird."

"I won't." She gave me another long look. "I guess I would give BDSM a try for a guy like that, too," she muttered to herself as she walked back in the apartment.

Andi covered her eyes. "I kind of told her everything. My sisters, too. I mean, I censored out—" she lowered her voice to barely a whisper. "All the really dirty stuff. I didn't tell her that. I also kind of started writing a BDSM section for the blog, and it's blowing up. It had a thousand hits yesterday."

"That's incredible," I said, squeezing her hand. "And you can tell Rachel whatever you want," I said. "I don't even care if you tell her how unbelievable the blowjobs you give are."

There was a loud thump and a muffled groan of pain from inside the room. Both seemed to come only inches from the wall we were standing beside.

Andi stifled a laugh.

"So you're really not going to tell me where you're taking your sisters?" I asked.

"Nope. It's super-secret, and if I told you, you'd want to come."

"Interesting. Well, I'll just have to find something fun to do on my own, I guess."

"Without other women, I hope?"

"Oh, there will be women. Tons of them."

I could tell she was trying to figure out if I was serious, but I decided two could play at that game. "I'll see you tomorrow, Wainwright."

33

ANDI

Aubria and Bree looked a little disappointed when they saw my grand plan was to take them to an aquarium. Bree perked up a little when I asked for bands to get us into the dolphin encounter. I'd honestly been wanting to do this again ever since coming here with Landon, and I knew my story hadn't done the place justice.

We walked around together, looked at the fish, skimmed the informational plaques, and even ate the same cheesy fries I'd shared with Landon.

Bree dipped one of her fries in ketchup and ate it in a single bite.

"That's kind of gross," I said. "Ketchup and cheese?"

"One word," Bree said. "Cheeseburger."

I rolled my eyes. "That's different. Like, would you dip a potato in mayonnaise and take a big bite of it? *No.* But potato salad is delicious."

Bree waved a fry at me. "You have no idea what I would or would not do with a potato and some mayonnaise."

"You know what I want to know?" Audria asked.

"Where to find an endless supply of medical cadavers to experiment on?" I asked.

She shot me a dry look. "That's not even the kind of research I do. So, no. I want to know if grandpa is going to try to force Bree and I into some screwed up sexual adventure, too."

I shrugged. "Maybe. Or maybe this whole thing was more about Landon than it was about me. I mean, he did say I'd get the hotel either way."

Bree looked thoughtful. "If he was just going to give us our shares of the hotel, why wouldn't he have done it already?"

"I'm not sure," I said. "But I can't imagine we'll have to wait much longer to find out."

"Hey," Bree said. "Can we go wait by the dolphin place early? I kinda want to see what I'm getting into. The idea of jumping into some huge tank of water with a dolphin is actually freaking me out a little."

"What?" I asked. "Dolphins are like the sweetest animal known to man."

"False," Audria said. "Dolphins are sexual deviants. They assault people all the time, violently humping them if given the chance."

I snorted. "You're making that up."

"Wish I was," Audria said nonchalantly. "Look it up yourself."

Despite Audria's warnings, we headed to the tanks early enough to see the group before us finishing up. The way the area was set up allowed us a perfect view as we crossed a ramp that circled one of the tanks. I saw a dark-haired man treading water in the middle of the tank with a smile on his face so huge and genuine that it took me a second to recognize him. "You've got to be shitting me," I said, half in awe.

Audria and Bree followed my gaze.

"Is that..."

"Landon," I said in disbelief. "The dorky bastard came here by himself because I told him I had plans with you two tonight.

He probably thought I'd never find out." I fought the temptation to shout out and embarrass him right away. The more I saw, the more fun it would be when he realized he had been caught.

The dolphin swam over to him, inverted on its belly, and let Landon grab both fins. With a few pumps of its tail, the dolphin was dragging Landon across the surface of the water on its belly. Landon was *laughing* with delight.

My sisters and I were all laughing so hard our sides hurt by the time he was done getting his little joyride. He stood on the ledge while a family and their young kids stepped up to take their turn. He was still smiling when his eyes wandered our way. We all smiled back sweetly, waving.

Landon's expression turned from a smile to an outraged scowl so fast we all started laughing again.

"I present to you, the dork dom," I said. "Deceptively cute and good natured, despite all attempts to seem broody and angry. At times, it does stupid, *very* stupid things, but the dork dom also is an expert in apologies, *among other things*. Furthermore—"

Audria stopped me with a look. "You realize how hypocritical it is for you to call him a dork, right?"

Bree hugged her hands together and smiled. "They deserve each other, Audria. It's really cute."

I smiled, even though Landon was still glaring in my direction. I knew he couldn't hear anything I said from where he was, but I did know Bree was right. In some twisted way, we really did deserve each other.

34

EPILOGUE - ANDI

~

Two Months Later

A<small>BOUT THREE MONTHS AGO</small>, I <small>LOST MY GRANDPA</small>. I <small>THOUGHT HIS</small> last gift to me was the Kindle. Instead, he had given me something far more precious. *Landon Collins.*

Granted, it was more accurate to say he had locked Landon and I in a cage and hoped we would learn to get along before we killed each other. Still, I had Grandpa Willy to thank for how things had turned out.

I couldn't help thinking how happy he'd be to see where my writing was taking me. My little column on Rachel's blog about BDSM had managed to capture some of those wandering visitors looking for "Rachel's Ass to Mouth." It turned out they were also willing to stick around and read a little bit of my trials and tribulations in the world of BDSM. Within a couple days, the trickle of traffic turned into a stream, then a river.

Rachel had practically forced me to take the hint and make my own blog to capitalize on all the attention.

I hadn't even begun to figure out monetization or any of those fancy business aspects of running a blog, but I did have my first real taste of what I'd always wanted. I had readers. I had eyes on my words and a voice that people cared about listening to.

In his own way, Landon had helped me to find that, and it was just one more reason to be eternally grateful.

I grinned to myself when I thought of him. He was working at the moment, but I knew we had a date tonight. A date at The Golden Pecker, and he promised to use these fancy new knots he discovered on me.

I did feel a little guilty living in my own slice of paradise. Grandpa's next video had appeared, and it would be an understatement to say all hell broke loose. But I'd learned that sometimes it takes an explosion to put two broken people together. And no, that didn't exactly make sense in a literal way. But hey, Landon was the king of terrible metaphors. I at least got to have one or two bad ones, right?

35

EPILOGUE - LANDON

∾

Three Months Later

ANDI AND I WERE IN CALIFORNIA FOR ONE OF MOM'S TREATMENTS. Given the relative chaos that broke out after dear old William Wainwright released his next video, it was probably a good thing.

With everything going on, Andi desperately needed the break. I didn't mind the away time, either. Kicking Sydney and Edward out of the club had led to the kind of exodus of members I'd feared. But I hadn't realized how many people who had reasons to hate Sydney and her father or Edward and his tactics were willing to join once the two were gone. In the end, profits had hardly dipped.

I was still waiting for some kind of unexpected disaster to arrive and sweep it all away. When Andi wasn't busy during the days, we got to spend time together. A few nights a week, she came to the club and explored the world of being my submissive even further. It felt perfect. But for the first time in my life, I thought there was a chance this little slice of happiness was the kind that was meant to last.

Andi was wearing one of her growing collections of ridiculous sweaters, even though it was getting to be far too hot for them, especially in California. This one was fuzzy, red, and had a big heart in the center that could be unzipped. Andi was way too entertained by her ability to hold all of our stuff "in her heart." She had stuffed it so full of keys, phones, and every other little thing she could think to carry that it looked like it was about to rip away from her sweater entirely.

She was reading something on her Kindle while we waited for mom to be let out of recovery.

"What is this one about?" I asked.

She tilted her phone so I couldn't see and gave me a guarded look. "What if I don't want you to make fun of me?"

"Then you'll tell me, because I'm not going to make fun of you. Even if you dove back into the world of tentacle monster romances."

She grinned. "Okay. Yeah. It's not that bad. I'm just reading a BDSM book. I was hoping to get some ideas to use on this guy I kind of have the hots for."

"Oh? Do I know him."

"Hmm. I could try describing him and see if it rings any bells. Tell me when to stop," she set her phone down and bit her lip so sexily I almost stopped her right there with a kiss. Instead, I waited patiently.

"Let's see," Andi said. "He looks kind of scary, like he might tear you a new one if you pissed him off. But he's actually a really sweet guy once you get past all the grumbling threats. And he likes to get really jealous of me when he thinks I'm going to be around other men, but he still trusts me. It just drives him crazy, and it's kind of adorable watching how hard it is for him. What else... Oh, yeah. He's got this trick he can do with a feather where he basically makes you come without even—"

I softly put my hand over her mouth. Andi either didn't realize or didn't care that the elderly couple sitting across from us had been listening in with growing interest. I flashed an apologetic smile to them, then looked to Andi, who was smiling from behind my hand.

"If I remove my hand, are you going to behave?" I asked.

She shrugged.

As soon as I pulled my hand away, she picked up where she left off. "He can make you come with it even though you can't feel a thing, it's the most bizarre and inten—"

I covered her mouth again, then somewhat gently helped her to stand and led her to a little side area off the waiting room. I spotted a small concession area and took her inside it.

"Hey," she said, gesturing to the room around us. "Remind you of anything?"

I nodded. "Except this vending machine just has chips. No Skittles."

"Well, I didn't come here for the Skittles."

"No?" I said, smiling. I reached out for her, but she ducked under my arms and went to the machine behind me.

"Pretzel sticks sound so good right now."

I glared at her back, then turned her around so I had her pressed up against the machine. "This is what I wanted to do the first time I saw you at the Wainwright hotel."

"Did your plan evolve from here, or was pushing up against me the whole shebang?"

"There was more," I said. I tilted her chin up for a kiss, but approaching footsteps made us stop.

A mom and her son walked into the small room. "No," she said, trying to pull him away. "I already told you we're not having chips for breakfast. There are eggs in the hotel room."

The little boy, who must've been about eight, struggled and

tried to pull away. "The nurse said they were eggs been a dick. I'm not eating that, mom!"

My eyebrows shot up. Andi looked back at me with the same, shocked and amused expression.

The mom grabbed the boy by his sleeve and yanked him down the hallway. "It's eggs benedict," she grumbled at him. "Do I need to get your ears cleaned?"

Andi snorted out a laugh once they were out of earshot. "I can't blame him. If I was a kid and someone told me they were going to feed me the eggs that have been a dick, I'd be pissed, too."

When my mom came out a little while later, she looked tired. We helped her back to the car and then to her hotel room, which she had chided me for spending so much money on. I didn't care, though. I wanted her to at least get a little bit of the life my father tried so hard to keep her from having after she cheated.

"Any good news?" I asked once we had her back in her room.

"That depends," my mom said. "Is it good when the tumors get smaller? I forget how that works."

We ordered in some takeout for lunch to celebrate the good news. I'd learned that it wasn't a total victory. With cancer, it felt like there was no such thing. It could always come back. With mom, it felt like it always *would* come back. I was proud as hell of her for fighting it the way she had every time, just like she'd fought for my brother and me.

We were working on a large container of lo mien noodles when my mom got a devious glint in her eyes. "So," she said, looking between Andi and me. "How long are you two going to make me wait for a grandbaby? Because, as you can both see," she said, making a show of looking more tired and slumping back in her chair. "I might not have much time left."

I slid my tongue across my teeth, then moved my eyes to Andi. She was watching me with an unusually thoughtful look on her face.

"This reminds me of an old western shootout," mom said. "Neither of you want to be the first to play your cards. *Hmm.*"

"I was just thinking you're supposed to wait until people are married to start asking them about children," I said.

"Oh, is that so?" mom asked. "I guess I just figured the way you two get along, that would be coming any day now."

Andi blushed now.

I wanted to throw a fortune cookie at my mom for cornering me like this in front of Andi. I cleared my throat. Instead of throwing the cookie, I cracked it open and tried to read the fortune to change the subject.

I frowned down at the words and then set the fortune aside, hoping no one had noticed. Andi snatched it off the table and read. "A family that brings new life also brings happiness."

"*Okay,*" I said, plucking it from her hand and setting it in the bag. "There won't be any talk of grandbabies because we're not even married yet."

"Yet?" Andi asked.

I stammered. "I just mean it's a little like putting the bull before the horns."

Both Andi and my mom were leaning in conspiratorially. *Damn women.* Yes, I was planning to ask Andi to marry me, just as soon as I wouldn't look like I'd lost my mind for asking her so soon. And *yes,* I'd already decided having kids with her was something I wanted so much it hurt. Again, none of that felt like the sort of thing you said out loud about a woman you'd only been dating for three months.

"I wonder how he's planning to ask," my mom said.

"Mom," I said. "Maybe you could just let us work things out naturally without trying to force it along."

She nodded sadly. "Yes. Of course. If only I had all the time in the world to wait for you two young lovers to figure things out."

"What is it you want, a proposal right here at the table?" I asked.

"I'm more curious about what Andi wants." She turned to look at Andi, who was watching most of the exchange in rare silence.

"I..." Andi said slowly, moving her eyes between me and my mom. "I think it's safe to say there will be babies in your future, Miss Collins. Lots and lots of babies." Her eyes were locked on me while she spoke.

One of my eyebrows twitched upwards. "Is that right?"

My mom dropped the fork full of noodles she'd been holding and practically ran into the huge bedroom of her hotel suite, leaving the two of us at the table. "Don't let me stand in your way, kiddos!"

Andi and I had a silent staring match for a few moments after she left.

"You want kids?" I asked.

"Only if you are the one who puts them in me."

A low, fiery hunger ignited in my stomach. "You want me to put a baby in you," I said slowly.

"Yes," she said. "But it's like you said. Putting the bull before the horns and all..."

God, I loved this woman. "You realize what you're saying, right?"

Andi nodded. "There's the obvious unspoken part, and then the fun part where we get to practice until you get around to doing the thing we seem to want to skirt around saying out loud."

I grinned. "Yes. I wouldn't mind a few more practice runs before we start trying for real."

Andi bit her lip, then did the world's worst fake impression of a yawn and stretched her left hand toward me, wiggling her ring finger around. She coughed. "It's-a-size-seven," she said, squeezing the words in between fake coughs.

I got up and pulled her into a hug. "You're the most ridiculous person I've ever met. And I love you for it."

"Do you love me for my other parts, too?" she asked.

I squeezed her ass. "Yes. Your ass is a work of art."

She pulled back and fiddled with my jacket. "Hmm. What else?"

"Your breasts could inspire sculptures."

She raised an eyebrow. "Cheesy. But continue."

I lowered my voice to a low growl. "And your pussy is fucking delicious."

She purred playfully. "*Oh my*, Mr. Collins. You're quite the devil."

"Keep tempting me, and a devil is exactly what you'll get."

Andi stood on her tiptoes, so her mouth was just beside my ear. Her words came in a raspy whisper. "I want you to put a ring on my finger. And then I want you to put two babies in my belly. *Twins*. One boy, one girl."

I chuckled. "My balls aren't a fast food restaurant, Andi. You don't get to place custom orders."

She slid her hand between my thighs and squeezed slightly. "If those boys know what's good for them, they'll take my damn order. Understand?"

"One boy, one girl," I repeated. "And a ring. Did I forget anything?"

Andi tugged me down to her face and kissed me. "A few more of those," she said.

PLEASE DON'T FORGET TO LEAVE A REVIEW!

Thank you so much for reading! Whether you loved the book or not, it would mean the world to me if you left an honest review on Amazon. I read every single review and take them all to heart, even on older books, so it's not just a great way to give me your feedback and help me improve, it's also one of the best ways to support me and help me find new readers.

This book was a little bit of an experiment in combining romantic comedy and BDSM, so I'm pretty terrified to start getting feedback, haha. But please, please let me know what you think. If it seems like a lot of you enjoyed this, I'll absolutely continue the Pecker series!

ROMANTIC COMEDY

THE GOLDEN PECKER

1. The Golden Pecker
2. ??? ;)

OBJECTS OF ATTRACTION

1. His Banana
2. Her Cherry
3. His Treat
4. His Package
5. Her Secret
6. Her Bush

ANYONE BUT...

1. Anyone But Rich
2. Anyone But Cade
3. Anyone But Nick (Release date: January 21)

CONTEMPORARY ROMANCE

SINGLE DADS
1. Single Dad Next Door
2. Single Dad's Virgin
3. Single Dad's Hostage
Note: Not a series, just books about single dads!

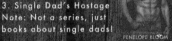

STANDALONES

1. Savage
2. Miss Matchmaker
3. The Bodyguard

BDSM

MAFIA

BABIES FOR THE DOMS
1. Knocked Up by The Dom
2. Knocked Up by The Master
3. Knocked Up and Punished

CITRIONE CRIME
1. His
2. Mine
3. Dark

Standalone BDSM
1. Punished
2. The Dom's Virgin
3. The Dom's Bride

1. Baby for the Beast
2. Baby for the Brute

Romantic Comedy BDSM
1. The Golden Pecker

Don't know where to start? I hope this helps!

STAY CONNECTED

Click the icons above for my mailing list and Facebook. Please check out my website and blog at www.penelope-bloom.com as well!

ALSO BY PENELOPE BLOOM

My Most Recent Books

Anyone But... Series
    Anyone But Rich
    Anyone But Cade
    Anyone But Nick (pre-order available)

The Objects of Attraction Series
    His Banana (top 8 Best Seller)
    Her Cherry (Top 5 Best Seller)
    His Treat (Top 6 Best Seller)
    His Package (top 7 Best Seller)
    His Secret (top 30 Best Seller)
    Her Bush (top 30 Best Seller)

Baby for the Beast (#60 Best Seller)
    Baby for the Brute (We don't have to talk about rank on this one, do we?)
    Savage (#20 Best Seller)
    The Dom's Bride (#40 Best Seller)

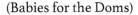

(Babies for the Doms)

 Knocked Up and Punished (top 21 Best Seller)

 Knocked Up by the Master (top 12 Best Seller)

 Knocked Up by the Dom (USA Today Bestselling Novel and #8 ranked Bestseller)

(The Citrione Crime Family)

 His (Book 1)

 Mine (Book 2)

 Dark (Book 3)

 Punished (top 40 Best Seller)

  Single Dad Next Door (top 12 Best Seller)

  The Dom's Virgin (top 22 Best Seller)

  Punished by the Prince (top 28 Best Seller)

  Single Dad's Virgin (top 10 Best Seller)

  Single Dad's Hostage (top 40 Best Seller)

  The Bodyguard

  Miss Matchmaker

Made in the USA
Middletown, DE
20 December 2019

81520231R00146